Praise for Nero Blanc's Crossword Murder Mysteries . . .

The Crossword Connection

"Another neat whodunit . . . Blanc builds the suspense slowly and surely, challenging the reader with a dandy puzzler."
—*Publishers Weekly*

"The denouement features some clever bait-and-switching with the suspects."
—*Kirkus Reviews*

"Intriguing plot . . . Keep[s] you guessing until the very end. The tension is carefully maintained and sustained . . . as you breathlessly wait for events to unfold."
—*I Love a Mystery*

Two Down

"[A] snappy, well-plotted story . . . Combines the best elements of the puzzle mystery and the village mystery."
—*Fort Lauderdale Sun-Sentinel*

"Engaging."
—*Publishers Weekly*

The Crossword Murder

"Evoe! At last puzzle fans have their revenge . . . super sleuthing and solving for puzzle lovers and mystery fans."
—Charles Preston, Puzzle Editor, *USA Today*

"A puzzle-lover's delight . . . A touch of suspense, a pinch of romance, and a whole lot of clever word clues . . . Blanc has concocted a story sure to appeal to crossword addicts and mystery lovers alike. What's a three letter word for this book? F-U-N."
—Earlene Fowler

"Designed to delight both crossword enthusiasts and mystery readers . . . Adroit word play and high society intrigue . . . [Blanc] delivers an enjoyable, complex solution and likeable protagonists."
—*Publishers Weekly*

"Addicts of crossword puzzles will relish *The Crossword Murder*."
—*Chicago Sun-Times*

Crossword Mysteries by Nero Blanc

THE CROSSWORD MURDER
TWO DOWN
THE CROSSWORD CONNECTION
A CROSSWORD TO DIE FOR
A CROSSWORDER'S HOLIDAY
CORPUS DE CROSSWORD
A CROSSWORDER'S GIFT

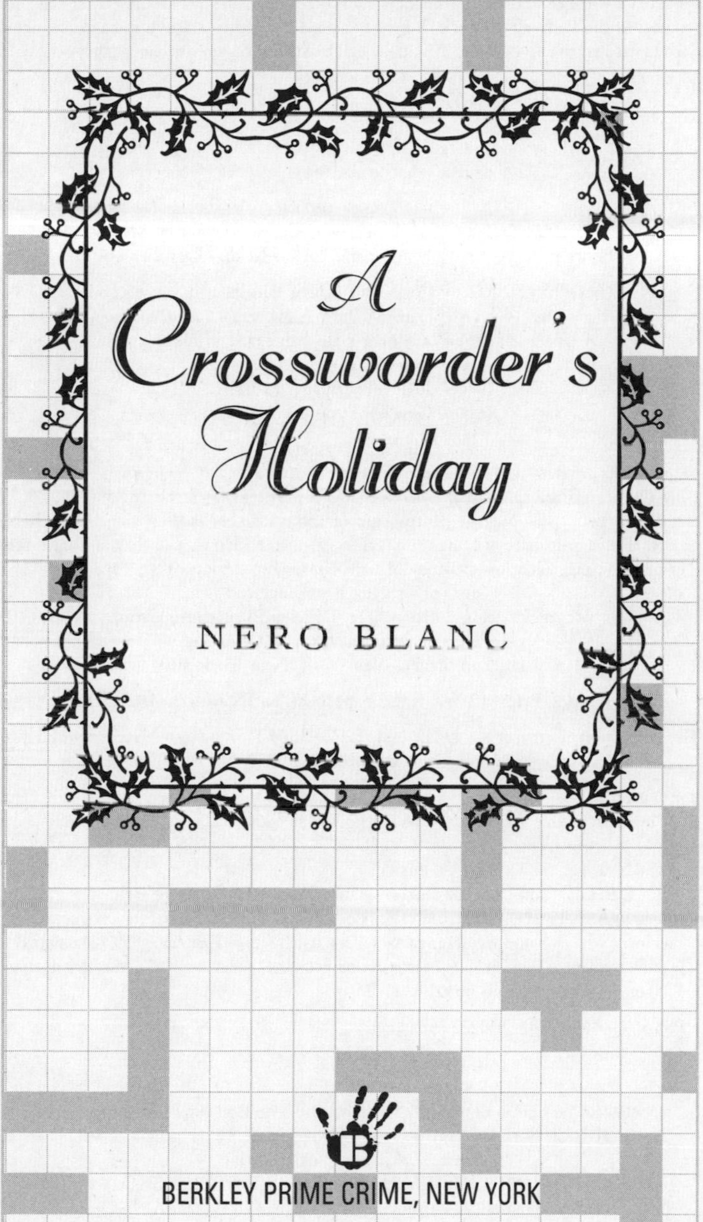

A Crossworder's Holiday

NERO BLANC

BERKLEY PRIME CRIME, NEW YORK

This is a work of fiction. Names, characters, places, and incidents either are the product of the author's imagination or are used fictitiously, and any resemblance to actual persons, living or dead, business establishments, events, or locales is entirely coincidental.

A CROSSWORDER'S HOLIDAY

A Berkley Prime Crime Book / published by arrangment with the authors

PRINTING HISTORY
Berkley Prime Crime hardcover edition / October 2002
Berkley Prime Crime trade paperback edition / October 2003

Portions of *A Ghost of Christmas Past, A Partridge in a Pear Tree,* and *A Crossworder's Holiday* originally appeared in *Hemispheres*.
Cover art by Grace DeVito.
Cover design by Judith Murello.
Text design by Tiffany Estreicher.

For information address: The Berkley Publishing Group,
a division of Penguin Group (USA) Inc.,
375 Hudson Street, New York, New York 10014.

Berkley Prime Crime trade paperback ISBN: 0-425-19260-1

The Library of Congress has cataloged the Berkley Prime Crime hardcover edition as follows:

Blanc, Nero.
A crossworder's holiday / Nero Blanc.—1st ed.
p. cm.
ISBN 0-425-18733-0 (alk. paper)
1. Detective and mystery stories, American. 2. Graham, Belle (Fictitious character)—Fiction. 3. Polycrates, Rosco (Fictitious character)—Fiction. 4. Private investigators—Massachusetts—Fiction. 5. Crossword puzzle makers—Fiction. 6. Crossword puzzles—Fiction. 7. Massachusetts—Fiction. 8. Crossword puzzles. I. Title.

PS3552.L365 C755 2002
813'.54—dc21

2002066660

Berkley Prime Crime Books are published by The Berkley Publishing Group, a division of the Penguin Group (USA) Inc., 375 Hudson Street, New York, New York 10014.
BERKLEY PRIME CRIME and the BERKLEY PRIME CRIME design are trademarks belonging to Penguin Group (USA) Inc.

PRINTED IN THE UNITED STATES OF AMERICA

10 9 8 7 6 5 4 3 2 1

A Letter from Nero Blanc

Dear Reader,

Curling up with a good mystery story is one of our favorite pastimes during the holidays. There's something about the dark days of winter that inspires the sleuth in all of us.

In this collection, we've created not just one but five tales. Each has a crossword that helps reveal the riddle; each features our fictional friends Rosco and Belle; and each comes with our very best wishes for a joyous holiday season.

We love getting letters from our fans and invite you to send your messages through our website: www.crosswordmysteries.com where you'll find information about other Nero Blanc books—as well as how we devised our nom de plume.

Super sleuthing and puzzle solving! We look forward to hearing from you.

Steve and Cordelia
AKA
Nero Blanc

The authors have dedicated a percentage of their earnings from this book to The St. Barnabas Mission in Philadelphia, Pennsylvania.*

*St. Barnabas Mission provides emergency shelter, educational and social services to homeless women and their children. The Mission is administered by Episcopal Community Services (ECS), a not-for-profit social service agency that has been helping people of all faiths for over 130 years. ECS: 225 South Third Street, Philadelphia, PA 19106-3910; www.ecs1870.org.

A Crossworder's
Holiday

"PLEASE, you must help me. I fear this day bodes extreme ill . . . Please . . . You're the only person to whom I can turn . . ."

Seated in the evergreen-draped dining room of a Nantucket inn while luxuriating over a second cup of coffee and an ever-present copy of *Moby Dick*, Belle Graham glanced up in surprise—mingled with a measure of annoyance. This was her vacation, after all, and she and her husband, Rosco, had come to the quaint Massachusetts island in order to escape just such interruptions. They'd intended this year's Christmas holiday to be a quiet getaway. No extended family. No scheduling conflicts. No beepers or cell phones or work piling up on the desk. Nothing, in fact, except sleigh bells, snow-laden lanes, houses bedecked for the season, and the broad, blue sea that gave the island its singular light.

"You *are* Annabella Graham, are you not? The crossword editor of the Newcastle *Evening Crier*?"

"Yes. I am." Belle executed a polite smile despite her irritation.

Her unwelcome visitor glanced apprehensively around the room. He was a tall, willowy-looking gentlemen, meticulously manicured but highly agitated—in fact, he seemed almost to quiver with fright. Belle guessed him to be about twice her age, probably in his late sixties. His accent and deportment were British and very much old school. Tweeds, a cherry-colored scarf, a soft woolen hat tossed nervously from hand to hand, and walking boots fresh out of the box completed the picture.

She toyed with her book, wiggling a finger into the pages to mark her place. "And you are?"

The question seemed to take him by surprise; his tone turned to one verging on desperation. "Oh, that's not . . . Well, of course, I should . . ." Again, the rapid perusal of the room's inhabitants. "Perhaps we could converse elsewhere . . . Mrs. . . . Miss . . . ? Or may I be so bold as to call you Annabella . . . ?"

"Belle," was her automatic reply. Although Annabella was her given name, its combination with Graham had early on inspired the nickname "Anagram"—a hybrid she avoided whenever possible. She cast a longing glance at her book, then swept her pale blond hair from her face. It was a habitual gesture, the act of an attractive young woman who views beauty as a poor second to brains. "I don't use Annabella. It seems to inspire too many 'Graham Bell' jests . . ."

The man stared in confusion.

"The inventor . . . Alexander . . ." Belle shook her head, realizing the quip was lost on the anxious Englishman. "And you are?"

He cleared his throat, appeared to make a quick decision, then lifted his chin in a motion that made him look as if he were seeking to escape from the starched collar that peeped out from beneath his scarf. "Sir Brandon Drake." The name was murmured in a swift, *sotto voce* rush. "Of Drake Antiquarians, Boston?" This latter piece of information was added questioningly as if the speaker hoped Belle would recognize the name. She did, of course; Brandon Drake was world-renowned as a purveyor of priceless Americana.

"And you're reading *Moby Dick,* I see," he continued in an equally breathless fashion. "Very appropriate for Nantucket . . . *The White Whale* . . . Inscribed to Nathaniel Hawthorne, you know, another literary genius of the young United States. 'In token of My Admiration for His Genius'—"

Belle stifled a sigh. "Is that what you wish to discuss with me, Sir Brandon? My choice in vacation novels?"

In answer, Drake rocked forward on his toes. "I'm not here alone," he murmured obliquely. "We arrived yesterday afternoon . . . all five of us . . ."

Belle suppressed a second sigh while cursing herself for a genetic inability to be rude to her elders. She stared at her congealing cup of coffee. "Would you care to sit down? I'm expecting my husband to join me shortly, and—"

Again, Drake leapt as though electrocuted. "Ah, yes, Rosco Polycrates . . . the private investigator . . . I've read about your dual exploits, which is why I . . ." Then the speaker's tone again dropped to a whisper. "I can't be seen here, and with five of us, there are bound to be, well . . . You and I are certain to be spotted . . ."

The reply did nothing to enlighten her, although Belle recalled that she and Rosco had noticed an unusual group of revelers clambering into the inn's reception rooms the previous evening: two women and three men. One woman had worn a wildly dramatic hat swathed in mauve and purple veiling; the other had literally jangled within a vivid array of Native American jewelry. The men had been equally noteworthy: one pale and bottom-heavy as a pear, one square and noisily robust, and Sir Brandon, the quintessential British country gentleman—replete with an "Oxbridge" accent.

Drake bent toward Belle's table. "I don't want them to notice us talking, you see." He cast a wary eye toward the inn's reception area, then surreptitiously displayed a slim, half-morocco slipcase, an object she recognized as designed to contain a rare book or valuable autograph. From within its interior, he withdrew a hand-drawn crossword puzzle. The paper was new, the answers blank. This was obviously not the article for which the slipcase had been constructed.

"I realize word games have many devotees—and techniques and rules of which I am sadly unaware," Drake continued as he concealed the crossword again. "Time is of the essence, as I will explain. I beg you to help me."

"But—" Belle began, intending to object that she and Rosco had every intention of keeping their vacation both private and puzzle-free, but Drake overrode her attempt at protest with a more stringent:

"I beg of you . . . of you and your husband, actually . . . I'm well aware of your reputation at solving—"

"We're here on vacation—"

"Please. Just this one small word game."

Belle silenced a private growl. *What I need,* she decided, *is to learn how to say no.* But then that resolution inspired a fleeting image of a bumper sticker replete with a crossword grid and a red banner slashing across it. CRAZY FOR CRYPTICS? WE CAN HELP . . .

"Okay . . . just this one. But my husband—"

"Of course," was Sir Brandon's conciliatory response. "I do not *remotely* intend to infringe upon your solitude."

Belle raised an eyebrow, but didn't otherwise respond.

CLIMBING the staircase to her bedroom, she found Rosco returning from his morning run, his face ruddy with cold and good health.

"Don't tell me you had breakfast without me?" A shocked smile lit up his dark eyes.

"I couldn't help myself." Belle grinned as she spoke.

"Let me guess . . . Cholesterol-hell . . . Pancakes, sausages, maple syrup—"

"Belgian waffles . . . But you're right about everything else . . . and blueberry jam *with* the syrup . . . and cocoa—not coffee—with *cream.*" Belle hefted her book in her hands while Rosco's questioning glance grew.

"And now you're going to say that you intend to sit up here reading Melville while I wolf down my share of culinary no-nos?"

"Not exactly . . ."

Rosco stared at her, comprehension finally dawning. "Someone found out you were here."

"Someone found out we're *both* here," was her hurried reply. She was about to add a facetious: *That's the price of fame,* but thought better of it. Sometimes that fame had unpleasant side effects—as the husband-and-wife team of private investigator and crossword editor had unwittingly discovered.

"I'm off-duty, Belle. So are you—"

"It's just one puzzle, Rosco—"

"I think I've heard that one before—"

"I promise."

"Mmmm . . . hmmm . . . and no murder victims this time? No corpse under the bed?"

"Absolutely not! At least, I don't think so . . ."

"Why doesn't that make me feel remotely comfortable?"

"Because you're of Greek descent, and therefore naturally given to high drama?"

"Because I'm reasonable."

"Well, I am, too . . . sometimes."

"It's not the *sometimes* that worry me."

Belle laughed as she reached for her coat. "I'm off to the Athenaeum, but I'll be back by the time you finish your buckwheat flapjacks."

"What makes you think I'm going to order flapjacks?"

She raised an eyebrow. "My *un*reasonable feminine intuition."

"And what, may I ask, is at the Athenaeum?"

"That's for me to know and you to find out."

THE sky was a brilliant, icy blue as Belle hurried down Centre Street, the sun's rays sliding across the houses' weathered shingles, making every doorway, every shutter, every bow-trimmed holly wreath appear in stark relief as if carved by the island's sea-washed light. Seagulls wheeled high overhead, and she could smell the sharp, salt tang of the ocean. In the midst of the bustling, winter town, she almost thought she could hear waves breaking upon the shore.

Then this mood of reverie carried her into the island's past. She imagined the rhythms of the seasons before the advent of automobiles and electricity: the ripening cranberry bogs resplendent with autumn's vibrant reds, the winters encrusted in whorls of ice, April finally bringing a thaw to the harbor, whose whaling ships would then depart for months or years at a time. And finally, the wives who waited, holding together family and village. A special kind of person had been spawned and inspired by this demanding climate: Benjamin Franklin's mother, Abiah, the reformist Lucretia Mott, and Herman Melville himself, with his discourse on whaling, lost innocence, and hellish revenge.

Belle was so transported by these meditations that it took her a moment to realize she'd reached her destination. She looked up at the library's white and curiously windowless facade, and whispered an awestruck: "Oh my . . ." For a lover of words, the building cast a palpable spell; none other than Ralph Waldo Emerson had dedicated it; and he and other *litterati* of the age, Thoreau, Daniel Webster, and John

James Audubon, had lectured in its noble second-floor Great Hall.

She entered, her copy of *Moby Dick* tucked in her handbag. The book seemed like a talisman, a tangible connection to the past. "What wonder then," Melville had written of the island residents, "that these Nantucketers, born on a beach, should take to the sea for a livelihood!"

It required concerted effort for her to recognize that the year was not 1851.

Belle found Sir Brandon already seated at an antique reading desk beneath an electrified oil lamp. "I am indebted to you," he announced as she approached. "My reputation rests on this seemingly unimportant scrap of paper. It's a matter of life and death." In response to her startled expression, he added, "Figuratively, I should say, although . . ."

"Perhaps you should begin at the beginning," was Belle's calm reply.

Drake sighed with the long, remorseful sound of a worried man. "My companions and I journeyed here to visit Timothy Hyde-Hare . . . You've heard of him, of course?"

"Should I have?"

"Perhaps not . . . perhaps not . . . Timothy is a reclusive, dare I say, eccentric fellow? He is also one of the world's great connoisseurs of art as well as an eminent—and exceedingly wealthy—collector. Every year he hosts a holiday weekend in one of his homes for five select antique dealers, his house here being that spectacular Georgian brick residence on Pleasant Street . . . As you can imagine, invitations are much sought after by those in the antiquarian trade. My four colleagues and I have been Timothy's guests for a number of years. The 'A' list, if you will . . . an admirable position, but not without risk . . ."

Belle frowned; her facile brain had intuited the uneasy truth behind Drake's words.

"I see from your expression that you perceive us to be sycophants . . ." Sir Brandon continued, his frame bending as if bearing the weight of her scrutiny. "And you are correct when you assume that we folk 'in trade' rely upon the largess of our patrons, however—"

Belle interrupted with a shake of her head. "What does your relationship with Hyde-Hare have to do with the crossword puzzle you showed me?"

"I'm coming to that," Drake answered a trifle stiffly. "As I said, Freda, Portia, Rolf, Ashe, and I have been

Timothy's hand-picked coterie for a goodly while . . . Portia Gibbons is not only famous for her *outré* hats, but for the rare and unusual Russian icons she purveys. Freda Karcher's forte is antique, Native American art; she can readily distinguish between the Santa Ana or Zuñi Pueblos. Rolf Peterssen—he's the rather rotund fellow—deals in Mogul paintings, specifically those charming domestic scenes of the Tanjore School. Ashe Saterlee is a connoisseur of silver, and has recently completed a monograph on George W. Shiebler; late-nineteenth-century design is Ashe's bailiwick. In short, we are all experts and considered such by our peers." Sir Brandon's defensive tone suddenly changed to one of camaraderie. "What do you know about the machinations of the art world?"

Belle's expression grew wary. With personal involvement in the arrest of the murderer of another noted collector, she knew far more about the art and antiques trade than she wished to. "I've heard the business described as 'brutal,' " she finally replied.

Sir Brandon didn't detect the reticence in her tone. "An understatement," he groaned. "Gallery owners, museum directors, and moneyed patrons can be a most bloodthirsty breed . . . One day, they treat you like the proverbial film star, jetting you hither and yon, champagne on private aircraft, invitations to 'redo' a ten-room 'pied-à-terre'; the next, you're a nonentity. For that reason my four colleagues and I fiercely guard our 'friendship' with Timothy. There are many waiting to take our places if we falter. And needless to say, our status affords us entrée to a charmed circle of the most affluent of collectors."

"But how does this relate to your crossword?" Belle's question had a challenging edge that Drake mistook for disapproval.

He paused and splayed his pampered fingers across the tabletop. "Timothy invented a 'game'—a yearly auction of five objects from a field in which neither I nor my friends have sufficient background to bid knowledgeably. It's Timothy's way of *tweaking* our pride, you see . . . The problem is that one of these articles is always a brilliant fake. When word leaks out—as it invariably does—that a member of our group has been, well . . . humbled, the gossip turns nasty—not to mention, competitive . . . You do realize that an antiquarian's 'marketability' rests on the buyer's belief in his or her experience. If a client is considering spending many thousands of dollars for a single item, absolute faith in the seller becomes imperative."

"I take it that this is your 'life-or-death' situation, then?"

"It may seem unimportant to you—this bartering over ancient objects, but when one's livelihood . . . one's very *name* . . ." Drake's voice trailed off. He sighed. "We arrived yesterday on the high-speed ferry from Hyannis: Portia first winging in from London, Freda from Dallas; Rolf and Ashe from Frankfurt and San Francisco, respectively, and I from Boston. After settling into our accommodations—if one of Timothy's homes cannot host us all, he provides a stellar alternative—we proceeded to his house for dinner. As on all previous instances, at the close of the evening, he conducted the auction. The only rules are that we discover the sham before the next evening—not an easy task in a remote locale such as this—and that we do not reveal our findings to each other prior to meeting again with our host."

"And you believe you are now in possession of Hyde-Hare's fake?"

Sir Brandon lowered his courtly head. "When I discovered the crossword puzzle hidden inside my purchase, I feared the worst. It would be typical of Timothy to employ a word game to reveal the truth.

I should add that none of my colleagues received any type of missive . . ."

Why submit yourself to such abuse? Belle wanted to ask, and as if Drake had read her mind, he continued:

"I must also confess that dealers and collectors share a secret vice—an inherent passion for gambling. The dusty little watercolor purchased for a few dollars in a rummage sale might prove to be a long-lost Winslow Homer, the badly tarnished silver ladle a genuine example of Paul Revere's extraordinary craftsmanship . . . So, yes, Timothy's 'game' can be as profitable as it is costly." A small, embarrassed smile formed on Sir Brandon's face. "I suppose you could say that the chickens constantly hope to outwit the fox."

Belle considered Drake's words as she made her decision. Discounting ordinary human vanity and ambition, there seemed nothing untoward in his behavior. "May I see the puzzle?"

Sir Brandon relinquished a sheet of graph paper that had become damp within his anxious clasp. Belle scanned the crossword with a professional eye, immediately recognizing that the constructor had created four fifteen-letter lines of the type traditionally employed for long quotations. A fifth, centered and shorter clue was part of the design. *QUIP, part 1*, 16-Across announced; 56-Across stated *QUIP, part 5*. Drake was quite correct in his assumption. The crossword contained a message.

"I happen to be quite skilled at reading upside down, and when I spotted your name in the guest register, I experienced a sudden ray of hope. As I explained, I have no facility with word games, but I'm well aware that many people are addicted to your column."

Belle smiled briefly at the compliment. "I don't know if I'd use as strong a term as 'addicted,' " she said before resuming her inspection of the crossword. "So, you're asking me to supply the answers?"

"If you would be so kind . . . and also . . ."

Belle looked up while Sir Brandon fidgeted nervously. "Also?"

"I beg you to tell no one of what you learn . . . I've never been duped before, you see, and I fear my reputation . . . My friends are more complaisant than I . . . Perhaps it's because they're younger and it's easier for them to laugh at misfortune. On the other hand . . ." His voice nearly broke. He was a very troubled man.

Belle changed the subject with a practical: "Could you describe the theme of this year's auction?"

"Manuscripts and autographs." Drake hefted the slipcase. "Herein resides an Ernest Hemingway letter, typed, signed, and dated April 9, 1931—along with a hand-addressed and stamped envelope bearing a cancellation mark of Key West . . . If genuine, it represents a unique piece of Americana, as well as being quite a bargain. Ashe purchased a letter from Sigmund Freud, signed 'Sigm.'; Freda pounced upon the title page of Margaret Mitchell's novel *Gone with the Wind*—supposedly signed by cast members of the film. Personally, I wouldn't have touched it with a ten-foot pole. To my mind, it had reproduction written all over it . . . Rolf grabbed an original, signed drawing by E. H. Shepard—the artist whose work is synonymous with the Winnie the Pooh series . . . while Portia fell for Rudyard Kipling's corrected typescript of *The White Seal* . . ."

Belle let Sir Brandon continue his monologue while her eyes raced over the puzzle. There were numerous references to Nantucket, and four clues alluding to Drake's companions. She reached into her purse and pulled out her trusty red pen. Even when filling in crosswords, Belle liked to throw caution to the winds. A pencil would never do. "I'll need help with this," she said. "3-Down is *SILVER COLLECTOR?* Can you tell me what that means?"

Sir Brandon looked panicky. "I don't believe there's a specific term," he began, but Belle interrupted him.

"What about your friend from San Francisco?"

Drake's relief was evident. "Oh, Saterlee," he said. "I see. You require his name."

"Four letters," was her patient response, to which Sir Brandon exclaimed a joyous:

"Ashe, of course! With an E, like the former tennis great . . ."

ASHE, Belle penned at 3-Down, then turned to 18-Down. *"GERMAN LAD?"* she asked.

"Rolf Peterssen."

Belle wrote ROLF, then pointed to 25-Down and 28-Down, adding PORTIA and FREDAS at Drake's suggestion. Then she looked at 51-Down: *The____ thickens*. "Ah, yes," she murmured while inking in PLOT, then suddenly remembered the time—and the fact that she had interests on the island that weren't exclusively lexical.

She stood. "Sir Brandon, I told my husband I'd meet him back at the hotel. I'll take this with me if you don't mind—"

"Oh, my!" was his unhappy response. "But I was hoping, well, that we could keep this to ourselves . . . at least for the nonce—"

Belle frowned. "If my husband can't be trusted, then neither can I."

"Oh, dear . . . I certainly didn't intend to imply that . . . well, oh dear me . . ." Drake shook his head. "Perhaps I might inveigle you *both* to take luncheon with me, and we could—"

"Sir Brandon, Rosco and I are here on vacation—"

"Of course . . . Of course, you are . . ." But instead of appearing apologetic for his intrusive behavior, Drake looked more alarmed. "I beg you to recall that time is of the essence," he finally murmured in what sounded like the whimper of a small dog.

Belle folded the crossword and began to put it in her purse, but Sir Brandon stopped her. "Then, perhaps you and your husband might join me for a preprandial libation? We could meet at the Chowder House on Straight Wharf. I've been advised that it's quite an island tradition. We could complete the puzzle then . . . Until that time, I believe it's best if I return it to the slipcase. I wouldn't want my companions . . ." He left the sentence unfinished.

* * *

"IT doesn't sound like this guy's on the up and up, Belle." Husband and wife were strolling down Main Street, their boots scrunching through dry and powdery snow while dustings of the feathery stuff blew in the breeze catching the sunlight in diamond-bright sparkles that billowed into the air. It was a scene almost too pretty to exist.

"I *thought* you'd say that," Belle rejoined with a pensive nod. "And I've got to say I tend to agree . . . All the same . . ."

Rosco chuckled. "*All the same,* you're hooked."

In response, a sheepish smile settled on Belle's face. "Well, you have to admit it's a curious story."

"But what if Drake's the one trying to pull a fast one? What if he believes that—? Do you mind describing those other items Hyde-Hare auctioned again?"

"Besides Sir Brandon's Hemingway letter, there was one supposedly from Sigmund Freud, the title page of *Gone with the Wind* signed by cast members from the film—"

"Clark Gable et al."

"I would have started with Vivien Leigh," Belle said with a chuckle.

"What about Superman? He was in it too."

"Superman?"

"The old one, the one on television—George Reeves."

"Really?"

"Uh-uh . . . What else?"

"Any more obscure film lore up your sleeve?" Belle smiled again, then returned to Rosco's question. "What else . . . A chapter from Rudyard Kipling's *The Jungle Book*, a Shepard drawing of Eeyore and Piglet. The Mitchell was the one Drake felt most dubious about—"

"That's just it," Rosco interrupted. "He all but pronounced it a fake, right?"

"Right."

"Well, what if he *knows* the Mitchell piece *isn't* a phony . . . but he's trying to convince everyone that it is. What if he constructed the puzzle himself—"

"But Drake knows nothing about crosswords."

"So he *told* you, Belle . . . just as he *supposedly* confided that Hyde-Hare hid the puzzle in the slipcase . . . Let's not forget that antique dealers are in the sales business. What if he's trying to sell you a bill of goods?"

"But what would Drake gain with his bogus crossword?"

"Well, this is just a theory . . . and it's not a very pleasant one . . . that your illustrious Sir Brandon might—I repeat *might*—have pegged you for a naive do-gooder, and decided to—"

Belle made a wry face.

"Well, you *are* a do-gooder. Just think about it for a minute."

"It was the *naive* part I'm objecting to."

"Okay, gullible. How's that?"

"Rosco, that's worse!"

"I didn't marry you for your manipulative, deceptive ways. It was strictly a *bod* thing."

Belle laughed. "You said it was my brain . . . Besides, if you think you're softening me up, dream on." She wrapped her mittened hand around his arm, and gave him a playful squeeze. "Okay, let's hear the rest of this hypothesis about how integral I am to Drake's sneaky ploy."

"Right . . . The Brit spots your name in the inn's guest register—upside down, according to him—then decides luck has fallen in his lap, nips upstairs, grabs a pen and paper, whips up a crossword, and—"

"I don't think your scenario works, Rosco. The puzzle he showed me is fairly advanced; constructing one takes time—"

"*You* could create one in a single night—"

"Well, yes, but—"

"So, who's to say Sir Brandon isn't equally adept?"

Belle nodded—albeit a trifle ruefully. "Okay, I'm with you."

"The next morning—today—while your husband's conveniently absent, Drake sidles up to you—"

"Being the aforementioned *gullible* do-gooder and crossword fiend—"

"Correct. Then, you do him a big favor and fill in the clues, thereby discovering that, let's say, the autographed Mitchell title page is a sham . . . After which, you decide to perform a kindly act, and tell the woman who 'purchased' it—"

"Freda Karcher."

"Right . . . You tell Freda—in the strictest confidence—and Drake soon appears on the scene murmuring condolences and offering to secretly take it off her hands and save further embarrassment . . . Maybe even trade for his Hemingway—"

"But all this time, the Mitchell is the genuine article . . ."

"Bingo."

Belle released a troubled breath, stepped off the curb, and almost collided with a horse-drawn sleigh. She looked up in surprise. "I have the weirdest sense of being thrown backward in time."

"You've been reading too many tales of the nineteenth century," Rosco said as he pulled her back to safety.

"The Mountebank Unmasked: or The Incredible Account of the Meretricious Manuscript."

"Something like that."

THE preprandial party got off to a rocky start. Rosco was on the lookout; Belle was tightlipped and increasingly wary, and their behavior immediately put Sir Brandon on the defensive. Nerves made him not only more voluble, but also more lordly and condescending: neither of which were favored traits with Rosco or Belle.

"The view is similar to one Melville might have enjoyed before shipping out on the *Acushnet*," Drake observed in his loudest and most British "public school" tone while the three seated themselves at a window table, and the antiquarian launched into a discourse of the world *Moby Dick*'s creator inhabited. "Do you know that in the early nineteenth century lobster was a staple of the poor man's diet? From Maine to Connecticut, a populace grown weary of the glorious crustacean while yearning all the while for the solace of stewed chicken—which was then considered a rich man's dish . . . Lobsters and oysters. Oh dear. Oh dear . . . Nowadays, we have 'boutique' bivalves and spiny creatures raised in roiling saltwater tanks. The world would do well to take a few lessons from history . . ."

Belle only half listened as she unfolded the crossword Drake had now returned to her.

"You've read Melville's *Etymology,* I take it?" Sir Brandon continued, glancing first at Rosco and then at Belle. "And *Extracts*—those extensive quotations concerning the great leviathan?"

" 'Very like a whale,' " Belle muttered. *"Hamlet."* Then she abruptly changed the subject. "5-Across needs three letters: _____*-Off Land; Nanticut.*"

"The word I believe you're searching for is FAR; that's what Nanticut means; it's the ancestral tribal name for Nantucket Island as Timothy so graciously explained to us . . . We're thirty miles out to sea, you know . . . Thus FAR . . ."

Belle's pen continued to bustle across the paper. "53-Across,: *Wauwinet to Jetties Beach dir.?*"

Drake thought a moment. "West-southwest would be most accurate, I imagine."

Belle said and wrote, "WSW," then added, "32-Down: *Surfside to Siasconset dir.*"

"That would be ENE . . . and it's pronounced 'Sconset,' by the way; Nantucketers don't believe in wasting unnecessary syllables."

"Considering you've never been here before, you seem to know a great deal about the island," Rosco observed.

Sir Brandon smiled benignly. "Oh, I have my host to thank for that." He looked at Belle. "Well? What have you found, my dear?"

"I'm not finished yet." Her eyes continued scanning clues and answers. 15-Across: *Tall____; lie*; 38-Down: *Slippery one.* Her foot nudged Rosco's under the table. Turning toward Drake, Rosco asked a seemingly guileless:

"What will you do if your Hemingway letter proves to be a phony?"

"I don't know," was the sad reply. "As I told your wife, I've never received one of Timothy's counterfeit masterpieces, and I've gotten quite a name in our close-knit community for my acumen." He sighed.

Stagily, Rosco thought. "You know the French painter Corot, do you not?"

Rosco nodded; Belle, with her eyes still on the crossword, also signaled assent.

"Well, the jest," Drake continued, "if one might call it that—is that in the artist's lifetime he executed some four hundred landscape paintings . . . eight hundred of which are right here in the United States."

Rosco stared, perplexed, then said, "Obviously an artist, and not a mathematician."

"Quite. You see, not all of those evocative oils signed Jean Baptiste Camille Corot are the genuine article. Many thousands, nay, millions of dollars have been frittered away on worthless canvases! Not only by Corot, but many others. As I told your wife earlier, a collector requires implicit faith in the person purveying a work of art."

"Are you saying your career would be ruined if Hyde-Hare tricked you?" Rosco asked.

Drake's answer was a weary: "Forgers are brilliant creatures; they give bronzes a patina of age; marble statuary can be 'distressed'; worm holes are added to wood . . . The techniques are myriad, and the criminal mind endlessly inventive. We, who count ourselves experts, must be able to discern the genuine from the sham. If not, well . . ."

"What does Hyde-Hare gain by this yearly 'auction'?" Rosco asked.

"The money from the auction goes to a charitable institution—a considerable boon for the fortunate recipient. Other than that, the event is a form of entertainment for a fellow who enjoys amusing himself over the foibles of human behavior. Timothy, well, how can I put this tactfully? You are familiar with the Bard?" Drake didn't wait for a reply, but instead quoted: " 'As flies to wanton boys, are we to the gods; They kill us for their sport.' *Lear* . . ."

Belle was only partially aware of this exchange. Words in the puzzle had begun to leap out at her: *Risk, Espy, Snare.* But who was at risk? Who should beware of the snare? She put down the crossword. "I'm afraid I'm momentarily stumped," she lied. "Do you mind if I take a breather, and finish later this afternoon?"

Drake's face reddened. "Of course . . . If you must . . . Don't want you exhausting yourself, my dear." The words tumbled from him in a staccato rush.

The three stood, Drake awkwardly attempting to pull back Belle's chair while she, as eagerly, tried to avoid further contact.

"I'll drop this at the hotel when I'm done." She forced another smile. "In a sealed envelope."

"Good of you. Very good of you, I'm sure. Very good of you both to donate your valuable time . . . I've made a reproduction on the hotel fax machine . . ." Sir Brandon added a small bow while Belle put the crossword in her purse, slipping it inside her copy of *Moby Dick*. She and Rosco turned to leave, then Rosco posed another question. "You're certain none of your companions received a clandestine message last night?"

"No one was supplied with any article other than that which he or she had 'purchased.' "

"Did you ask them?"

"I had no need to query anyone, Mr. Polycrates . . . I've spent more than half of my life in auction houses, and have become a keen observer of human quirks and feints. When a competitor seeks to bid against me surreptitiously, I recognize the action immediately."

Belle added nothing to this exchange. *Risk, Espy, Snare*, her brain repeated. "I'll bring you the finished crossword this afternoon, Sir Brandon," she said instead.

* * *

"HE'S guilty of something, I'll put money on it," Rosco pronounced as he and Belle—without Brandon Drake's company—finished a leisurely lunch.

"You don't like him because you think he's pompous." She chortled as she reached across the table and took her husband's hand.

"*Pompous,* hah . . . Queen of the Understatements!"

Belle laughed again, then looked toward the restaurant's windows. The glass near the mullions was frosted, the red and white checked curtains swagged in greenery and strands of shiny Nantucket cranberries. Candles scented with bayberry burned on every table top. "Let's not go home," she said with a happy sigh.

"Permanent holiday or permanent Christmas?"

"Either one . . ." Then her brain, as was typical, leapt to an entirely new train of thought. " 'Your whales must be seen before they can be killed,' " she said.

"Come again?"

"It's a line from 'The Mast-Head,' a chapter in *Moby Dick* . . . I told you Drake made a huge point of my choice in reading material. He went on and on about Melville over drinks, too . . . I wonder why."

Then before Rosco had time to protest, she'd grabbed her purse and retrieved Sir Brandon's crossword, spreading it across the tablecloth while a waitress appeared, removing empty dishes and reciting a sunny: "Today's desserts are New England apple crisp, cranberry cobbler, candied ginger upside-down cake, and Indian pudding."

"Fine with me," was Belle's distracted response.

"I think you're supposed to pick *one*—" Rosco began, but his wife was too absorbed to notice.

"The first part of the *QUIP* . . . *part two, three, four* . . ." Suddenly she sat back and spun the completed crossword around so that Rosco could also decipher the message. ". . . Start here . . . and finish here . . ." Her fingers anxiously tapped the paper as he read. "Well? What does that say about your conspiracy theory? And Sir Brandon?"

"Hmmm . . ." He nodded. "So, where do we go from here?"

"You mean right this minute or later?"

"Both."

"Well, I'd say our first responsibility is to dive into a big bowl of Indian pudding."

ACROSS

1. Fence part
5. _____-Off Land; Nanticut
8. Mast
12. Watch brand
14. _____avis
15. Tall_____; lie
16. QUIP, part 1
19. Espy
20. _____Chaney
21. Turf
22. Beeper
24. Fra_____Lippi
28. QUIP, part 2
33. Having mystic writing
34. Charged particle
35. Computer memory
36. JFK stats.
37. QUIP, part 3
39. "_____risk to you"
40. _____Pérignon
41. Yank's opposite
42. "Moby Dick," et al.
43. QUIP, part 4
48. Fr. Junipero_____; Calif. missionary
49. Sobs
50. Chinese "Red;" abbr.
52. Zuider_____
53. Wauwinet to Jetties Beach dir.
56. QUIP, part 5
62. "Or_____!"; ultimatum
63. Unique
64. Navigational tool
65. Summer drinks
66. Rat-a-_____
67. Head of France?

DOWN

1. H.S. courses
2. Bride's veil
3. SILVER COLLECTOR
4. Spanish aunt
5. Trend
6. "Trim the yard_____"
7. Flying fish?
8. Atelier
9. Buddy
10. Whaler's quaff
11. Hotel booking; abbr.
13. Ashore
14. Subscription option
17. Type of dancer
18. GERMAN LAD?
22. CEO, often
23. Pot o' gold indicator
25. ICON LADY
26. 1918 Nobelist
27. Change, as water
28. KARCHER AND OTHERS
29. First down at Shea?
30. A Latin lover?
31. Mythic Arabian bird
32. Surfside to Siasconset dir.
37. Royal inits.
38. Slippery one
39. Spring mos.
42. Owl & Pussycat creator
44. Gothic touches?
45. Dip chip

A Crossworder's Holiday

46. Clam type
47. Soda type
51. "The_____thickens!"
53. Get your feet wet?
54. Card game
55. Type of wolf?
56. Affirmative vote
57. Not young
58. Employ
59. M.E. evidence
60. Fish snare
61. _____cat

The Proof of the Pudding . . .

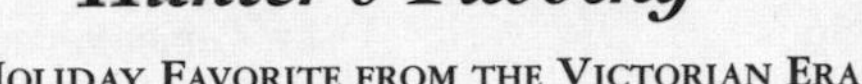

Hunter's Pudding

A Holiday Favorite from the Victorian Era

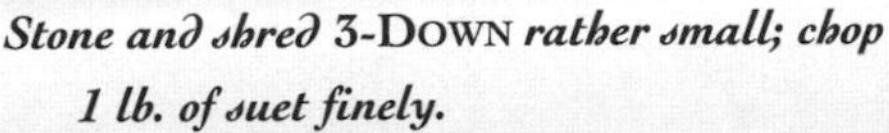

Stone and shred 3-Down *rather small; chop 1 lb. of suet finely.*

Pound 1/2 of 23-Across, *6 of* 54-Across, *and 2 of* 58 Across *into powder.*

Rub 1 lb. of stale bread crumbs until the lumps are well broken.

Cut 1/4 lb. of 18-across *into thin strips.*

Chop 1 lb. of currants.

Blend all these ingredients well . . .

Add 1/2 lb. of sugar and 1 tbs. of flour.

Beat 8 eggs to a virgorous froth; while beating, add 10 drops of 38-Across *and 10 drops of essence of lemon.*

Fold the egg mixture into the dry ingredients; mix and add 27-Down.

Tie the pudding firmly in a cloth.

Boil for 6 hours (7 or 8 would be better yet).

Serve with boiled custard, red currant jelly, or brandy sauce.

Sufficient for 9 or 10 persons

ACROSS

1. Building addition
4. WWII flyers
7. Bumbler?
10. 10-10; e.g.
13. Women's____
14. "The Greatest"
15. Everything
16. Countdown ender
17. Odysseus' rescuer
18. PUDDING PART
21. Sam____
23. PUDDING PART
24. Soil; comb. form
25. Rest room sign
26. Creams
30. It's often not admissible
32. Favorite
34. Caucho tree
35. ____Stravinsky
36. Monopoly purchase; abbr.
37. Once follower
38. PUDDING PART
42. Greek letters
43. ____Amin
44. Ego
45. Charged atom
46. Small piece
47. Defendable
50. Bill____
52. Christmas tree often
53. Russian river
54. PUDDING PART
57. Hold off
58. PUDDING PART
62. Fall mo.
63. "____All in the Game"
64. Squabble
65. Common conjunction
66. Dr.____
67. '60s grp.
68. Draft org.
69. Tide movement
70. Over there

DOWN

1. Prophet of Kings
2. Article length
3. PUDDING PART
4. Tear
5. King lead-in
6. Albert____
7. Worms often
8. Pre H.S.
9. Firstborn
10. Digit
11. Chemical suffix
12. Slippery one
19. Dough demand
20. Golf org.
22. Pushes ahead
25. ____Gay Harden
27. PUDDING PART
28. Western Canadian prov.
29. Post
31. Like father, like____
32. Trial print; abbr.
33. Error eliminator
36. King of France
37. Dot the O's?
38. "Ben-Hur," e.g.

The Proof of the Pudding

1	2	3	■	4	5	6	■	7	8	9	■	10	11	12
13			■	14			■	15			■	16		
17			■	18			19				20			
21			22		■	23						■	■	■
24				■	25			■	■	26		27	28	29
30				31			■	32	33		■	34		
■	■	35				■	36			■	37			
38	39					40				41				
42				■	43			■	44				■	■
45			■	46			■	47					48	49
50			51		■	■	52			■	53			
■	■	■	54		55	56			■	57				
58	59	60							61		■	62		
63			■	64			■	65			■	66		
67			■	68			■	69			■	70		

39. "Scat"
40. _____"Kookie" Byrnes
41. _____Cariou
46. 10th President's family
47. Aromatic tea
48. Work in Italy
49. Not quite a dozen
51. A&E link
52. Not masc.
55. Tic-Tac-Toe winners
56. Some posts; abbr.
57. Certain Slav
58. Altar material
59. Relative of Inc.
60. Fool
61. Kernel keeper

TONIGHT'S recipe cover was created especially in your honor." It was Frank Finney, the handlebar-mustachioed owner of Vermont's Misty Valley Inn who said this, although he retained a proud—almost triumphant—possession of his offering.

"A crossword puzzle . . . with a recipe for Hunter's Pudding, as you'll note. It was a great favorite—a staple, one might say—of the Victorian holiday table . . . The artwork and cookery instructions were devised by one of our frequent guests, Mrs. Stacy Lavoro, a longtime member of the other party here . . . We shall miss her and her husband, but their regrettable last-minute change of plans enabled the three of you to join us in their stead. And for that we are eternally grateful." With that, the inn's magisterial host produced the recipe, handing them around to the threesome at the table before turning his attention to the dining room's only other inhabitants: a rather noisy party of six.

"But how—?" Belle began.

"—did someone manage to construct a crossword on such short notice?" It was Sara Briephs who finished the sentence. As surrogate grandmother to the younger woman, as well as a blissfully unrepentant autocrat, the octogenarian felt it not only her right but her duty to come to Belle and her husband's aid—whether the assistance was requested or not.

As Belle regarded Sara, a smile crept into her eyes. "That's *not* what I was about to say, Miss-Know-It-All. I was going to ask how anyone knew Rosco and I—and you—were visiting. We were on a *waiting* list, after all."

"Well, I assume the guest who canceled . . ." Sara paused, her carefully coiffed head suddenly lifting in concern. "You're right, dear; revealing the identities of visitors does seem rather a breach of etiquette . . ."

Rosco, wisely, kept his eyes intent upon the menu's contents during this exchange.

After a moment Belle added, "Oh, I get it now," and glanced at her husband. "This has nothing to do with missing guests—or even a recipe hidden in a crossword . . . There's a secret message in the puzzle. It's going to say, 'Happy Birthday, Sara. December Twenty-eighth'—"

"I certainly hope you didn't tell them that my birthday's the day after tomorrow, dear child—"

"*I* didn't," Belle continued, "but someone *else* at the table might have spilled the beans." She nudged Rosco's foot with her own. "Fess up."

He raised his hands over his head. "Don't look at me."

Belle laughed. "It's a terrible thing not to believe your spouse."

"Really . . . It's the truth, Belle."

"What do you think, Sara? Butter wouldn't melt in his mouth."

"I'd say he's innocence itself."

"Inculpable," put in Belle. "A paragon of virtue."

"Pure as the driven snow, a brick, a trump . . ."

"I've never heard that one."

"Before your time, dear child . . . Derived from triumph, I might add." Her bright blue eyes twinkled; her patrician face wreathed with glee.

"You win," laughed Belle, but the two women's customary linguistic sparring was cut short by an uncomfortably loud argument that arose from the room's other table: one couple in the party of six seemed unable to keep their rancorous feelings private.

"We can discuss this later, Marcia."

"It's *late* enough already, Gene—if you want to know." The voice had taken on a tone of inebriated and reckless abandon.

"I meant upstairs in the privacy of our room." The words were a basso hiss of malice.

"Oh, why not air our dirty laundry with the group, honey bunch? They're your best friends, aren't they? Your dearest, dearest buddies in all the whole wide world. They're the reason we troop up here every damn—"

"Marcia, please—"

"*Marcia, please,* my foot. Since when—?"

"Hey, you two," a raucous male companion called out. He was in his early forties, expensively decked out in the very latest in country weekend garb, and his tone was full of forced cheer. "Kiss and make up . . . Then let's get on with our host's most excellent feed."

Another male and two other females joined the exhortation. Like their companion, they also appeared to be in their forties and were equally expensively groomed and accoutered. "Kiss and make up, Marcia, Gene . . ."

The inn's host reappeared at that moment, moving effortlessly among the residents of the argument-stricken table. "An *amuse buche* for Marcia . . . *pâté aux truffes* for Gene . . . white asparagus from Holland . . . a soupçon of ceviche . . ."

"They must be serious foodies," murmured Belle.

"They are," Rosco answered. "The host warned me we were in for a 'culinary roller coaster' when our rooms became available two days ago. Apparently, the same group comes up here every year during the holiday season; after the first night, they take over the kitchen and whip up all sorts of surprises."

"As long as they don't whip each other," was Sara's wry comment.

DINNER progressed, an endless array of goodies, cooked to perfection—so Belle, Rosco, and Sara surmised by the delighted comments from the neighboring table. No more rancorous outbursts marred the festivities; in fact, a decided peace had descended on the place—the various dishes served blending seamlessly with equally pleasing surroundings: the traditional painted paneling of a historic Vermont country inn decorated with greenery and tartan bows, starched lace curtains tied with crimson velvet ribbon, a fire flickering upward from the stone hearth while beyond the windows the blackness resonated with comforting solitude.

Not a single far-off porch lamp was sighted, not a car's high beams bounced by in the distance, not a plane's flickering lights intruded. The nine guests at the Misty Valley Inn, their hosts Frank and Agnes Finney, and Lori, the young woman who helped out as kitchen maid, parlor maid, and chamber maid, might as well have been dropped into a private and sybaritic sphere.

"Happy?" Rosco asked as he leaned toward his wife.

Belle nodded. "Aren't we all?"

Sara cleared her throat. "I'll let you two lovebirds continue to bill and coo, while I repair to my room and trundle off to the land of nod." She started to push back from the table, but Belle reached out a hand to stop the older woman.

"We don't want you to go, Sara. This is your celebratory weekend . . . Besides, you haven't tasted the Hunter's Pudding yet . . . the much-vaunted recipe—"

Sara's reply was a tart: "Have you ever eaten Hunter's Pudding?" She looked at Rosco.

"Something tells me it's not high on your list . . ."

"Oh, it's tasty all right . . . *Very* tasty . . . My grandmother made it . . . Her grandmother boiled it up before her—and probably *her* grandmother before that . . . But it's definitely not a low-cal treat—"

"You have to live a little, Sara. It's your birthday." Belle laughed.

"I already have, my dear. I already have. And that's why I—" But Sara's protestations were interrupted by the ceremonious procession of the Finneys and Lori bearing a flaming Hunter's Pudding aloft into the room. "Happy birthday . . ." they sang while Sara whispered an inaudible, "It's not until the day after tomorrow." Then she turned to the window, noticing before any of the inn's other residents that it had begun to snow. Her face creased in an expression that mingled both joy and regret. " 'The season of snows and sins' . . . Swinburne."

"A poet long before *your* time, Sara." Belle took the older lady's hand. "Besides, what happened to 'pure as the driven snow'?"

"Touché, dear girl."

* * *

DURING the night, Sara was awakened more than once with abdominal pains and a slight case of the chills. Being a "mind over matter" New Englander, and a devout believer in physical exercise, she finally got up, pulled her woolliest sweater over her flannel robe, and began pacing her room, all the while criticizing herself for overindulgence in the previous evening's feast. It was the pudding, in particular, that bore the weight of her ire. She was too old a lady, she decided, to be filling her gullet with rich foods.

"Besides causing bad dreams," Sara said aloud, then smiled in the dimly lit room. It was the voice of her long-dead father she heard. Her father who had espoused the notion that nightmares were the product of fats and sugars improperly digested. Apple pie slathered with ice cream was high on his list of guilty comestibles. And floating island, and plum cake with hard sauce. As a child, Sara had paid only lip service to the dire parental warnings.

Feeling a trifle better, she removed her sweater, folded it carefully, then returned to bed. Within a few minutes she was fast asleep. But her brain was full of disquieting visions. She imagined she heard whisperings outside her door, imagined she heard furtive footfalls creaking past, imagined the snow had grown so deep that the roads had vanished, that the inn was cut off from the rest of civilization.

Then Sara dreamed she heard a woman screaming, and awakened to find it was true.

"DEAD . . . He's dead!" It was Marcia, the argumentative wife of the previous evening, now distraught and sobbing spasmodically while Frank and Agnes Finney tried to calm her as the other members of the party hurried bleary-eyed from their rooms. "And I was . . . I was . . . Oh, my God . . . the last words I—!"

Rosco arrived on the scene followed immediately by Belle. "What happened?"

Frank Finney pointed toward the bed. "I'm afraid Mr. Jaffe—" while Marcia screeched out a tear-shaken:

"It's Gene . . . He's . . ." She gazed goggle-eyed at the prone figure of her husband, his rumpled pajamas and tangled sheets, the glass of water lying spilled on the nightstand. "I told him he should go on that diet! Over and over, I told him! The doctor said so, too. . . ." Her words flew out in bumpy gasps. "With his cholesterol . . . risk of a heart attack . . . He must have . . ." Marcia buried her face in Agnes Finney's protective shoulder and wept afresh.

Rosco, ever the P.I., eased his way over to the bed and assessed the situation. The deceased's eyes were wide open; the hands clutched the bedclothes, and a look of horror had frozen on the face. It was true that Gene Jaffe was no longer among the living, but Rosco guessed that coronary disease hadn't been to blame. He decided to keep that opinion to himself for the moment, however. If Jaffe had been murdered, the criminal was too close for comfort.

"Look here," a male member of the group said while he strode farther into the room. It was the same man who'd initially taken charge during Marcia's outbreak the evening before, and he now confronted Rosco with the belligerence of an accepted leader. "Our party needs a little solitude here. The lady's—"

"I'm a private investigator and former police officer, and until we contact the Vermont authorities—"

"The authorities!" Marcia shrieked, tottering forward until it looked as though she were about to collapse on her husband's body. One of the other women in the group pulled her back. She was clad in a flame-colored velour dressing gown that matched her flame-colored hair; genuine concern seemed to emanate from her. "Oh, Bobbi . . ." Marcia wailed while Rosco turned to Frank Finney:

"Is there a local constable you—?"

"I appreciate your sense of decorum, Mr. Polycrates. But the snow seems to have knocked out the phone lines. Agnes just tried to reach an ambulance service—"

"I'll get our cell phone," Belle offered while Rosco returned his gaze to the body on the bed, and then gradually took in the fact that the other bed hadn't been slept in, and that the new widow was swathed in blanketing.

At that moment, everyone else crowded into the room appeared to notice the same thing, and there was an uneasy shuffling of slippered feet as Marcia, again trying to control her fear and shock, began to speak. "Gene and I . . . You all know we had that itsy-bitsy little blowup at dinner . . . and then, well, he was kind of in his cups . . . I mean, weren't we all?" She looked beseechingly around the room. Blank faces gazed back. "So, I decided . . . well, you know what they say about arguing when under the influence . . . So, I thought I'd just curl up by the fire downstairs . . . and sort of let the heat up here cool off . . . And then I guess I dozed off . . ."

Again, she looked to her friends, who again ignored her unspoken pleas. "After I woke up, I thought I'd just creep back and climb into bed . . .'Cause I thought, you know, that Gene and I could kiss and make up in the morning. But, but—" She began to sob anew.

"So you only entered the bedroom a few minutes ago, Mrs. Jaffe?"

All faces swiveled toward Rosco, then swung back toward Marcia as though they were watching a tennis match.

"Well, you know how Gene can be when he—" She bit her lip; her chest rose and fell. "No, I guess you don't . . ." Her voice dropped to a near whisper. "Yes, yes, I slept downstairs . . . All by my lonesome . . ."

The guest who'd first addressed Rosco took the lead again. "Look, Polycrates—or whatever your name is—I don't know why you're here, but it's obvious that Mrs. Jaffe is in a highly agitated state . . . She needs sympathy and care, not an interrogation. None of us do. Gene Jaffe was both friend and colleague—"

But Rosco was not to be browbeaten. "And you are?"

"Sacks . . . Chuck Sacks . . . Charlotte, my wife," he added as an afterthought, indicating a woman in a black dressing gown trimmed with glossy maribou feathers, then waved his hand to indicate the third couple who made up the party. "Bob Tyler and his wife, Bobbi—"

Belle reappeared at that moment, silently handing Rosco the cell phone; who then diplomatically passed it to the inn's host.

The room was silent while the emergency call was made, and the death reported. Finney flipped the receiver shut. "There's been a car wreck," he said. "On the other side of the covered bridge. A bad one. No one can get through until they cut the driver out and a tow truck moves the vehicle—and someone assesses structural damage to the bridge. We've been advised to sit tight."

"Not much else we can do in the middle of the night, in the middle of a snowstorm," observed Bob Tyler. His mouth was hard. He shrugged. "Sorry, I'm just being practical."

"The night is darkest just before the dawn." It was Sara who offered this bit of homespun wisdom. She smiled sympathetically as she spoke, the very image of an old woman with a heart of gold and demeanor to match. "Why don't we all go downstairs and have some cocoa. It's a comfort in terrible times like these to feel that one is not among strangers." She looked at Belle, who glanced at Rosco; all three nodded in private collusion while Sara moved to Marcia Jaffe's side. "I'm so sorry, my dear . . . I'm a widow myself . . ."

Marcia said nothing.

STILL in their robes, the residents of the Misty Valley Inn sat clustered in front of the fire in the first-floor parlor. Lori and Agnes passed around mugs of cocoa and coffee, which some sipped at but no one truly drank.

"Cosby's Coffee," Chuck Sacks announced in a tone that was overloud and overebullient. "I'd recognize the taste anywhere."

His black-clad wife snorted, and grasped her coffee mug so tightly her vermilion-colored nails looked like bloodied talons. "Can't we talk about something other than business, business, business?"

"C'mon, you two—" began a sincere Bobbi Tyler, but Charlotte fixed her with a withering stare:

"Are you telling me you enjoy discussing—?"

"You wouldn't have that new fur coat you were dolled up in yesterday if it weren't for—"

"Cosby's Coffee?" Sara supplied the words. She'd

been sitting near Belle and Marcia, and idly penciling in answers to the crossword recipe. "You mean, *the* Cosby Café chain? Are you young people connected with that extraordinarily successful enterprise? Why, your attractive shops are all over the country. Almost on every street corner."

Bob Tyler answered. His voice had an aw-shucks openness. "Founders and partners. At least, we men are. Started the business back in our college days. Harvard, of course."

The smile was a little too smug for Rosco, but he said nothing as Tyler pushed on:

"Small time—a way to earn a little extra dough. We all roomed together, but by senior year we'd picked up an apartment in Cosby House, so the name kind of stuck. It was Gene who supplied our start-up capital; Stan's the bean counter . . . No pun intended."

"Well, isn't that wonderful!" Sara said. "And you've been good friends since then."

"Some of us," was Charlotte's steely reply.

"Hon," her husband began, but she retaliated with a waspish:

"I suppose you've conveniently forgotten what Gene announced last night—"

"This isn't the time—"

"Oh, stop it," moaned Marcia. "Gene loved everyone here. You know he did! Besides, if you hated his idea so much, you should have spoken up."

None of the others responded, and the remark echoed with ominous portent through the quiet room while beyond the still-dark windows the snow fell and fell and fell.

"38-Across," Sara mused, "*PUDDING PART* . . . Oh, I see, it's ESSENCE OF ALMOND . . ."

Belle looked at her friend while the old lady returned the glance, adding a sly and subtle wink. "My young friends and traveling companions are married," she said at length. "Rosco, as you've surmised, owns an investigative agency; Belle is none other than Annabella Graham, the crossword editor of Newcastle, Massachusetts's *Evening Crier*. It was for her sake that your missing friend created this marvelous crossword recipe—"

"That would be Stacy Lavoro," put in Bobbi Tyler.

At the mention of the name, Marcia gave a violent shudder, but Sara appeared to overlook the intensity of the reaction. "Cold, dear? Of course you are. You've had a terrible shock . . . Why don't you move closer to the fire?"

Dry-eyed, Marcia did as she was told while Sara calmly turned the crossword toward her. "And here's your name, dear . . . JAFFE at 21-Across and MARCIA at 25-Down. Wasn't that sweet of your friend to put you in the puzzle?"

Again, a conspiratorial glance passed from Sara to Belle while Marcia hunched her shoulders into a taut and bitter line and failed to reply.

DAWN came, and there was still no sign of the town constable—or of a plow. Rosco took Frank Finney aside, suggested that the dead man's room be put off-limits, but didn't allude to his suspicions. However, the inn's host obviously understood the gravity of the situation; in turn, he relayed his own hopes that the guests show respect for the deceased and allow the room to be locked. No one batted an eye at the request, and Rosco and Belle went back upstairs to carry out the plan.

"Surgical gloves?" Belle asked in a whisper as they reentered the Jaffes' room. "Since when do you pack surgical gloves for a vacation?"

"Since the last time I used the suitcase for an investigation, and didn't remember to *un*pack them."

"I take it you don't think we're looking at coronary disease."

"Astute as always—"

"My middle name." Belle pulled a pair of driving gloves from her bathrobe pocket, and dangled them in front of Rosco's eyes. "Let it not be said that I venture off on holiday weekends ill prepared." She donned the gloves. "Do you think Sara's okay?"

"You mean left alone with Charlotte Sacks, the snake in fancy feathers?"

Belle shook her head. "What I mean is this is almost Sara's birthday . . . It's not exactly what you'd call a festive atmosphere." They both stared at the bed where Jaffe lay.

"I wouldn't worry, Belle. You know how much Sara likes being in the thick of things—"

"Well, she's got her wish. A dead man . . . and a bunch of warring friends." Belle sighed. "This was supposed to be a quiet weekend getaway . . . a special celebration just for her . . ." The words trailed off.

"Sara's nobody's fool, Belle . . . and she's not the kind of person who expects life to be one continual party. In fact, I wouldn't be surprised if she isn't busy prying guilty secrets from that crowd downstairs."

Rosco walked to the head of the bed. "Jaffe was obviously struggling when he died . . ."

Belle drew in another troubled breath, then again shook her head as if to clear her brain and banish further concerns over her elderly friend. "Couldn't that have been the result of sudden heart failure—as Marcia suggested? He wakes up from a sound sleep . . . a lot of booze in his system . . . experiences palpitations, maybe severe chest pains, and tries to call out for his wife, but she's not here—"

"Possible . . . But there's something unnatural in this guy's pose . . . in his expression, too. I may be playing devil's advocate here, but I have a strong hunch that Jaffe was killed . . . asphyxiation, I'd guess . . . although there aren't any marks on his throat to indicate he was strangled . . ." Rosco bent closer to the body. "He could have been smothered by a pillow."

Belle thought. "Smothered . . ." Again, she shook her head, and repressed an additional sigh. "Well . . . what about an undiagnosed allergy . . . to nuts, or something like that? And he went into anaphylactic shock—which might look a lot like asphyxiation . . . I had a high school friend who couldn't get within twenty feet of almond extract."

"And so this is all a tragic accident?"

Belle nodded, her eyes serious. "Rosco, I just can't imagine one of these people snuck out of bed in the middle of the night, crept along the corridor, and slunk into this room."

"Slunk?"

"You'd prefer slank? Slinked? Anyway, he—or she—would have to have been aware that Marcia was curled up downstairs . . . Besides, this is an old building; nearly every floorboard and step creaks. Someone would have heard something . . ." A chill ran up Belle's spine. "If Jaffe *was* murdered, that means the killer is still in the house, sipping cocoa and Cosby's Coffee, and pretending—"

"What about Marcia?"

"Rosco, the woman's a basket case." Belle added a soft, "I would be, too . . ."

Rosco nodded. "I understand what you're saying, and I sincerely hope you're right . . . But a voice in my brain keeps insisting we're looking at homicide." He picked up the overturned glass, stared at it, then sniffed it. "I'm not detecting anything unusual, but a poison could present as a violent reaction—like heart failure or a food allergy . . . It wouldn't take much."

"The perfidious pudding."

"Don't joke, Belle. We all ate it."

"I know."

IT was on the stair landing that Belle paused to look out the window. The snow had ceased and morning had officially arrived, but the sky remained leaden and threatening. She gazed at the drifts so freshly formed, at the evergreens shrouded in white, at the inn's drive and car park, which had disappeared save for the guests' and owners' vehicles looking like so many ice cream boats topped with whipped cream. As the window began to steam up, she wiped it with her sleeve, then suddenly gasped.

"What is it?"

"Snowshoe tracks."

Rosco followed her glance. "Entering the rear of the inn . . . no, entering one of the attached outbuildings . . . walking *in*—not *out.*"

Both craned their necks to see further.

"Unless the person used another exit, we've got ourselves a visitor," Rosco said.

* * *

"YOU mean a visitor in addition to you and our other guests? There's another person here?" Frank Finney stared at Rosco in utter bewilderment. They were removed from the rest of the party, and talking in hushed, tense tones in the service pantry.

"Belle and I examined every view from the second-floor windows. The snowshoe tracks come toward the inn; they don't walk away."

"But who would come up here during a storm?"

Rosco decided it was time to take Finney into his confidence. "I have reason to suspect that Jaffe may not have died from natural circumstances."

The inn's host didn't speak for several long minutes. Rosco could see his shoulders droop, and his carefully groomed mustache twitch with an effort at courage and resolution before sagging into nervous dejection. "I can't afford that kind of publicity. It's bad enough if a guest dies under normal conditions . . ." He looked at Rosco again, his once ruddy cheeks pale and slack, his princely demeanor crushed. "Are you suggesting a murderer found his way up here, and is hiding somewhere among us?"

Rosco didn't supply an answer to the question. There was no need. Instead he said, "Do you know if Jaffe had enemies who wanted to see him dead?"

"You'd have to ask his wife or his friends. I only knew Gene as an affable guest—a once-a-year guest. I gather last night's festivities witnessed some unpleasantness pertaining to a joint business venture. I believe Gene was planning to sell out to the Moon-Bean chain, but that's as much as I know."

"If someone entered surreptitiously, are there places to hide?"

Finney gave a defeated groan. "In an old building like this—with the barn attached to the house, with the root cellar attached to that? There are places even I haven't fully explored yet." He shook his head slowly. "This is a nightmare."

Rosco thought. "Do these particular guests always opt for the same accommodations during their visits?"

"You mean, would an outsider be able to learn which room the Jaffes use?"

Rosco nodded while Finney's brooding silence gave Rosco the information he did—and didn't—want.

"Yes," Finney finally admitted. "They always take the same room—as the guest register indicates."

It now seemed logical that the killer had entered one of the attached outbuildings, crept into the residence, found the Jaffes' room, then retreated to his hiding place. How this person had intended to avoid

Marcia, Rosco didn't know. Unless the party's first evening at the inn was always an overly bibulous one; and well oiled with wines and cordials, the group was notorious for sleeping through anything.

However, what to do with this theory was unclear. Should Rosco share his concerns with the other guests and risk pandemonium? Say nothing and risk the possibility that the criminal might reappear?

"Is it possible to seal off the outbuildings so that no one can come in or out?"

"There are entrances on each floor—including the cellar."

"Do the doors have locks?"

"Old-fashioned brass ones."

"Let's hope they still work." As a seeming afterthought, Rosco added a cheerful, "By the way, is there any of that terrific Hunter's Pudding left over?"

Finney looked chagrined. "Sorry, no . . . I finished the last of the crumbs when I was cleaning up last night."

"But we each have a copy of the recipe, right? I mean, if we wanted to recreate the experience?"

"That's right. I followed it to a tee."

* * *

RETURNING to the parlor, Rosco found the group even edgier and more hostile toward one another, and Sara's placid puzzle solving seemed to only exacerbate the situation. "Look at this," she said brightly to Belle. "Here's a reference to COSBY at 50-Across . . . and SACKS—why, that must be Charlotte and Chuck—at 26-Across."

"Let me see that." Charlotte barreled across the room, the feathers of her dressing gown flying into her open mouth and sticking to her lips until she was forced to spit them out. "Where's my name?"

"Oh, and here's LAVORO at 48-Down," was Sara's calm reply.

Charlotte grabbed the crossword. "Where does that so-and-so get off putting *my* name in a puzzle?"

"You *and* your husband, dear."

"And what's this stuff about COSBY?" Charlotte wheeled on Marcia while throwing the word game to the floor. "Did the Lavoros know in advance what that creep husband of yours was planning to do? Were the four of you aiming to cheat us?"

"Hon . . ." Chuck Sacks cautioned although he began eying Marcia Jaffe intently.

"Gene thought you'd all be thrilled with his idea!" Marcia finally offered, her voice a wisp. "Your stock value would have been—"

"Tell me another funny story!" Charlotte snorted as she reached down and grabbed Marcia's arm. "Is that why Tad and Stacy canceled out at the last minute . . . 'cause they were waiting for you to drop this bombshell?"

"I don't know why they canceled," Marcia fought back. "And I don't care, either."

"Why, look at that," interrupted Sara at the window. "Snowshoe tracks walking toward the inn. What a perfect winter's scene."

Belle winced; Rosco winced while the feuding Tylers, Sackses, and the forlorn Marcia Jaffe all hurried to the old lady's side.

"Who made 'em?" Naturally, it was Chuck Sacks who spoke first.

"I would imagine our host or our hostess," offered Sara, "checking to ascertain potential damage during the—"

"How come they're just walking toward the inn and not around it?" Sacks argued.

"You probably need to ask Mr. or Mrs. Finney."

But at that moment a collective and frightening insight seemed to dawn. "Someone coming in and not going out . . ." Bobbi Tyler said in the barest of whispers, then suddenly turned around to face Rosco. "What if Gene was murdered?"

Rosco was ill-prepared for the question, but Belle replied with a reasonable: "Sometimes a violent allergic reaction can present an appearance of asphyxiation—or if, as Mrs. Jaffe suggests, her husband had coronary—"

"Gene was strangled?" Marcia yelped.

"I didn't say that—" Belle began, but Charlotte cut her short with a ghoulish:

"And that 'someone' is still here . . ."

"Oh, my God!" Marcia screamed, then flailed her arms, snagging Rosco's shoulder. "Get the police! Get them up here! Get them up here *now*!"

"We tried that already, Marcia," Frank Finney said as he walked into the room. "Remember? There's been an accident near the bridge."

"But . . . but—" was her near-hysterical response while Chuck Sacks barked a sharp:

"Let's calm down, everyone. Let's pull ourselves together . . . We don't need an outside private eye making a difficult situation worse. Maybe Gene died of an acute allergic reaction as has been suggested . . . or maybe it was heart failure like Marcia said . . . but it wasn't homicide, I guarantee you that. And we can't let ourselves get into a lather imagining we've got some crazed killer lurking among us." He turned his attention to Belle, obviously deciding she was more reasonable than her husband.

"You're the crossword expert, right? So, I take it you figured out the recipe for last night's pudding?"

Belle nodded.

"Well?" Sacks demanded. "Anything unusual in it? I mean any ingredient that might provoke a fatal reaction?"

"I'm not an allergist, Mr. Sacks. I'm a crossword puzzle editor . . . Offhand, though, I'd say that none of the ingredients seemed life-threatening—unless Mr. Jaffe had developed a sensitivity to nuts; in which case the presence of essence of almonds—"

"Gene wasn't allergic to anything," Marcia insisted. "Not nuts or anything!"

Belle turned her attention to Frank Finney. "You made the recipe according to Mrs. Lavoro's instructions?"

"Precisely."

"And there wasn't any additional substance you—?"

"I used only what Mrs. Lavoro called for." The inn's host had grown defensive and stiff. "It's not in my best interest to make my guests ill, let alone kill them."

"But if the mixture was left sitting on the kitchen table, someone else could have inserted another ingredient?"

"Obviously, Miss Graham. But in that case, I would imagine we'd all be facing Mr. Jaffe's fate."

Sara didn't speak although she distinctly recalled her discomfort the previous night. Unconciously she gripped her stomach.

"What about the brandy sauce?" Belle continued.

"Are you suggesting I poisoned a guest, Miss Graham? Because if that's the case—"

"No one's suggesting you did anything," Rosco interjected while Sara, still at the window, added a pensive: "Those snowshoe tracks look decidedly odd . . . The weight doesn't appear to be on the toe portion as it should be. It appears to be on the heel. Do you think . . . ?"

The tense band of friends paid no heed to her remarks; instead they began scrutinizing Marcia afresh, recalling in increasingly vivid detail the dead man's convulsed body, the overturned water glass, the wife who claimed she'd been absent when her husband had been stricken.

"Don't look at me like that!" the widow ordered. "None of you know what was going on between Gene and me."

Belle studied Marcia, then thoughtfully picked up the crossword again. Suddenly her eye caught a message no one had noticed. It ran across the diagonal, left to right, bottom to top. She stared at Gene's wife. "Why would Stacy put this in her puzzle?" Belle pointed to the hidden words.

For a long moment, Marcia's sole response was a frozen, almost vacant stare. Then her immobility turned dervishlike. "It's not fair! She can't even let me alone now! And how am I supposed to feel—with her writing trash like that?" She jabbed at the crossword. "That's all it is—just trash!"

"And Stacy's husband, Tad?"

"What about him?"

"What does he know about this?"

"Who cares what he knows or doesn't? Besides, why do you think those two didn't bother to show?" Marcia all but shouted while Chuck Sacks broke in with an irritable:

"What's going on here?"

But further explanation was curtailed by a harsh mechanical noise coming up the inn's drive.

"A snowplow," Sara observed. "Followed by a state police car."

"I didn't kill my husband!" Marcia Jaffe screamed. "I didn't."

"Then who did?" Rosco asked.

THE police officer's report dealt the group another blow. The vehicle involved in the accident near the covered bridge had been driven by none other than Tad Lavoro—who'd survived, but was in critical condition. At the scene he'd been hallucinatory, ranting incoherently as the fire department raced to extricate him from the mangled car.

"He seemed to be in one heck of a hurry," the state trooper added. "Never a good idea in this weather—and in the dark."

He went on to explain that, as a paramedic had worked an IV into the back of Tad's hand, she'd heard what she believed to be a mumbled confession; of Tad suffocating a man who had stolen his wife. A pair of old-fashioned snowshoes had been found on his car's rear seat.

"He must have used the pair I kept in the shed," the inn's host concluded. "They belonged to my grandfather—"

While Sara interrupted with a decisive: "I *thought* those tracks looked peculiar . . . Tad must have come to the inn early, before the snow grew heavy. By the time Gene was in bed, the snow had become impassable, so our murderer strapped those contraptions on his feet backwards . . . thus walking *out* while appearing to walk *toward* the inn . . . Well, well . . . Wasn't it Jung who said, 'The shoe that fits one person pinches another; there is no recipe for living . . .'?"

"Touché," was Belle's admiring reply.

A Partridge in a Pear Tree

FOR SALE. Rosco spotted the sign a full block and a half from the old, but immaculately maintained house. The highly colored and geometrically decorated placard was exactly how his former college buddy, Steve Sutter, had described it in his letter. "Remember, we do things differently down here in Bird-in-Hand. We're Pennsylvania Dutch through and through—right down to the old-fashioned lettering on our real estate signs. No cell phones . . . No e-mail . . . Yet. Folks around here may be practical, and they may be hard-nosed when it comes to business, but they don't like the look of 'modern' and they probably never will."

Rosco agreed with the assessment; his drive through rural Lancaster County had allowed him ample time to notice how intent each resident was on forestalling the pernicious winds of change. Dairy barns still proudly bore old-world hex signs; teams of woolly mules pulled wagons along unpaved farm lanes; plain, gray-black Amish buggies were led by high-stepping horses; smoke from hardwood fires rose from stone chimneys; tidy laundry lines abutted each house: the black trousers, shirts, and dresses worn by a traditional Lancaster County family flapping stiffly in the cold winter breeze. While settling around every house corner, every furrow in the plowed and now-barren fields, lay thin ribbons of snow, so white they looked like frosting on a new-made cake. Yes, it was a picture from another era.

But just as Rosco considered the charms of the world he was now entering, an enormous tractor-trailer sounded its air horn, then barreled past, roaring twenty-first-century impatience at the sleepy town.

For sale, he told himself. *For sale.* This wasn't going to be an easy visit. But then, things hadn't been particularly easy—or pleasant—in the old house for some time.

He drove across Maple Avenue, and parked in front of the venerable brick home that had once belonged to Steve Sutter's aunt. Miss Meg, as she'd been affectionately known, had been a village institution, once as famed for her gregarious wit as for her caramel-glazed *schnecken*. Miss Meg, born in this house to a father who'd also been born here—an entire line of Sutters: grands, great-grands, cousins, and siblings, all congregating within these walls for as long as anyone could remember.

Rosco stepped onto the porch, reflecting back fifteen years to his days at U-Mass—and then his first visit to the tiny town of Bird-in-Hand. He and Steve had been polar opposites in school, and unlikely friends: Rosco, the hard-nosed poli-sci major, grandson of Greek immigrants who'd disembarked in Boston Harbor and never left coastal Massachusetts—and Steve, a BFA student whose family tree extended over three hundred years to the German settlers who'd first begun farming this bucolic region of Pennsylvania.

What the two men had shared was a firm belief in right versus wrong—albeit in a college sort of way, and their friendship had survived despite different careers in very different locations. After serving as a police officer in the city of Newcastle, Massachusetts, for eight years, Rosco had segued into the private detective line; while Steve, on the other hand, had become a master carpenter and builder of fine furniture. His studio in Bird-in-Hand had garnered a national reputation, and he'd married a local woman, also a crafts person, and also of Pennsylvania Dutch descent. Hannah was as renowned in the field of quilt design as her husband was in turning a piece of mahogany.

Rosco knocked on a paneled front door that looked as ancient and scrupulously preserved as the house itself. The door flew open a few seconds later. "Hey, buddy! Thanks for coming down on such short notice. I owe you one." Steve Sutter beamed. His laconic manner, full, sandy brown beard, wire-rimmed glasses, and rumpled plaid shirt stood in stark contrast to Rosco's urban hustle and bustle. Rather than a handshake, Steve gave Rosco a large hug, and Rosco stiffened slightly at the intimate gesture. *Not a New England thing,* he thought, then: *Yeesch, these artists . . .*

"Sorry to hear about your aunt Meg's passing," he said when he was finally released.

Steve didn't answer for a moment. "A blessing . . . I guess that's what some people would say." He paused. "You remember her from the old days: fun-loving, sharp as a tack, a real pillar of this community. She knew everyone's name—even knew their great-grandmothers' names. But that's not how her life ended. The doctor over in the hospital in Lancaster referred to it as dementia . . . said it wasn't uncommon in people her age. Meg used to call it 'fate' . . . But it's tough watching someone who was once so vital . . . and the symptoms came on so fast—" The words broke off. Even so, Steve attempted another smile for his friend's benefit.

"It can happen that way . . . And sometimes it's people like your aunt who lose their will to live quicker . . . Maybe it is better she didn't linger."

"That's what I've been trying to tell myself."

The two men stepped into the parlor. Like the home's exterior, like the village itself, it was the product of another era: early American settles, Lancaster County dower chests lettered in German, candle stands painted with the traditional Pennsylvania Dutch *distelfink*—the good luck goldfinch. On the walls hung dozens of framed needlepoint samplers and *frakturs*, the records of births and baptisms intricately spelled out in colors as rich as autumn leaves.

Rosco stared at one sampler. "I don't remember seeing that one before . . . OEHBDDE." He read the letters aloud. "Is that a word? Because if it is, I've never seen it before."

Steve smiled softly, memories dancing deep in his black eyes. "It's German . . . An acronym, I guess you'd call it . . . OEHBDDE stands for *O Edel Herz Bedenk Dein End*. Translation: 'Oh, noble heart, consider your end.' It was Meg's favorite sampler. It used to hang in her bedroom, but she had me move it into the parlor near the end when she couldn't negotiate the stairs very well. Said she wanted to be reminded of its message every minute of the day."

Both men remained silent for a moment, then Rosco attempted an upbeat, "Belle would be in seventh heaven surrounded by all these letters and words." He looked at a dower chest boldly painted: BARBARA ANNO 1782, and an 1833 sampler in which the alphabet had been painstakingly stitched among birds and woodland animals. "She'd start seeing hidden messages . . ."

"I'm sorry she and Meg never met. They would have hit it off like house-afires . . ." Steve's words trailed off.

"Why don't you bring me up to speed on the latest developments," was Rosco's attempt at an unobtrusive response.

Steve took a long and troubled breath. "Nothing new to report . . . Just what I told you over the phone.

But I still want to contest Meg's will . . ." He raised his hands, anticipating Rosco's objections. "You know how much she loved this house, and how much she loved sharing its history. Before she took ill, she'd sit on the front porch, talking by the hour . . . Any passerby was her friend . . . Heck, she'd even flag down tourist busses and invite them to stop on over . . . Then she'd give each and every visitor the entire history of the community and of this house . . . She could tell you where each of these pieces originated. The OEHBDDE, for instance, was made by a great-great-great-aunt way back in 1832. Meg wanted this place to stay in the family—"

"Look, Steve . . ." Rosco interrupted, scratching at his chin as he spoke. "Don't you think a probate lawyer would be a better person for this job than a PI?"

But he remained firm. "You're an old buddy, and Meg liked you. The Pennsylvania Dutch put a good deal of trust in community. I don't want to deal with someone I've never seen."

"Contesting a will ain't easy, my friend."

"You told me that. And I appreciate your honesty . . . But I feel it's my duty as the last remaining Sutter living in Bird-in-Hand to keep the house and collection together . . . I feel it's my duty to *Meg*. It was the one thing she wanted. She said so over and over—and over again."

"But she—"

"Let me back up for a minute . . . I told you my aunt's will originally named her brother Amos as beneficiary?"

"Right . . . But that he predeceased her."

"By only four months, in fact. His passing was totally unexpected. A real shock for the entire community, not just family."

"I remember you telling me that when it happened," Rosco interjected, then waited for Steve to continue his tale.

"Well, a few days after Uncle Amos's death, Meg said she was creating a new will . . . She was going to leave the property and its contents to me—knowing full well it would remain intact." Steve paused. "But you know how it is when old people start talking about their own deaths . . . It's uncomfortable, and it's sad."

Rosco only nodded.

"Anyway, my response, whenever she brought up the issue of revising her will, was to tell her I didn't want her having gloomy ideas like that. I said Amos's death was just a terrible accident, and she was going to live to be one hundred or even more—which everyone in the town believed . . . But she always found a way to sneak her worries into our daily chats . . . She said she needed to 'safeguard the future' and make sure the place didn't 'fall into the wrong hands' . . ." Again, he paused. When he resumed speaking, his tone had turned pained. "And then, I don't know . . . she just fell apart. You wouldn't have recognized her, Rosco . . . All the old spunk was gone, and then her brain . . ." Steve's voice broke. "I mean, it was weird how quick she went."

Rosco nodded again, more in sympathy, while his friend shook his head sadly.

"What was really peculiar was that she was in great shape for nearly a month after Uncle Amos's passing . . ." He drew another troubled breath. "Meg was a great gal. I wish I'd paid more attention when she started talking about wills and things. Maybe she had a premonition she was going to die. Maybe instead of doing the hearty 'you're going to outlast us all' routine, I should have been more attuned to her fears . . ."

Rosco didn't answer for a moment; when he did, his voice remained low-key. "You did what you believed was best."

"I try to tell myself that—"

"It's tough . . ."

"The guilt's the worst."

Rosco tried a lighter tone. "Hey, come on . . . Your aunt wouldn't have wanted you to feel guilty, you know that, not in a million years."

But Steve's shoulders sagged. "I know," he said, clearly unwilling to lighten up.

Both men were silent while Meg's home, as if in sympathy with their feelings, echoed with the quiet sounds of all empty houses: a creak on the stair, a shift of a floorboard, the winter wind in the chimney flue, a clock still wound, still counting out its lonely minutes.

It was Steve who finally broke the mournful spell. "I know I'm tackling the impossible—"

"I wouldn't say *impossible*," Rosco responded. "But it sure ain't gonna be easy . . . So, there's definitely no evidence of a new will, I take it?"

"None whatsoever . . . When we spoke on the phone, I mentioned that everything's controlled by Amos's third wife, Greta—and I mean *everything*. Hannah and I call her Greedy Greta. 'Take the money and run' is definitely her motto. That's why Meg's collection is about to be packed up and sent to a New York auction house. After that, Greta intends to sell the house. 'To the highest bidder,' she keeps saying. And she doesn't give a hang whether it remains standing or succumbs to the wrecking ball."

"But why would anyone want to tear the place down?"

"The street's zoned commercially. It happened a long time ago—when the Farmer's Market went in. Back then, the townsfolk thought commercial was the way to go: local produce sold locally, and all that . . . Now, everyone's beginning to worry . . . Real estate's gotten real valuable around here . . ."

Rosco released a frustrated sigh and dropped his hands into his pockets as he looked around the room. The exposed beams had been hand-hewn, the wide floor planks lovingly polished, and every object seemed to embody the town's credo of honest work and wholesome living. "You're not painting a very optimistic scenario about Bird-in-Hand's future."

"It's the truth, though, Rosco. Every one of these small communities in Lancaster County is facing the same challenges. The same threats, I should say."

Rosco nodded. "And I'm sure this collection contains some seriously valuable items."

"You can say that again . . . Greta's positively got dollar signs dancing in her head."

"No 'visions of sugarplums,' huh?"

"Not unless the plums are prunes." Despite the gravity of the situation, Steve gave a brief laugh, then crossed to a painted sideboard decorated with unicorns and tulips, and opened the center drawer. "You know, my aunt had a lot in common with your Belle . . . Take a look at these." He pulled out a stack of crossword puzzles clipped from various newspapers. "Meg was a puzzle fanatic—had a shop in Lancaster mail her out-of-state newspapers. And even at the end, with her memory blinking on and off, it was her favorite hobby . . . Needless to say, the auction house isn't interested in my aunt's completed word games."

Rosco perused the puzzles. "Wow . . . Here's one from 1952 and another from 1969 . . . and here's one from a 1948 *Philadelphia Inquirer*." He squinted at it. "Huh? Thomas Dewey and Harry Truman both have eleven letters in their names. Did you know that?"

"Don't get started; you'll never stop . . . Meg liked to tell me she was as fascinated with the shapes of letters and words as I am with pieces of wood. Speaking of which, I should close up my shop on the way home. Hannah warned me not to be late. She's making her famous chicken *bot boi* for you."

"And shoofly pie?"

"You're not going to leave Bird-in-Hand hungry, that's for sure."

* * *

ROSCO and Steve walked through the snow-laced village. The sun was setting, and its salmon-colored rays reflected vividly off the icy white, bathing each house in lush pink and gold while the smells of home cooking perfumed the air: potato bread, apple fritters, and the sharp tang of sauerkraut. The chilled air seemed to make each aroma, each image, more pungent and compelling. The scents and sights filled Rosco with peace: small-town America settling into a cozy December night. Steve, however, bundled into his parka, his hands thrust deep in his pockets and his beard buried in a scarf, grew increasingly melancholy.

"When I was a kid, I used to walk along this very street on my way home from sledding. Everything looks the same as it did then; it even smells the same . . ."

Rosco let his friend's sorrow linger in the night air before speaking. "The town's going to lose something very important if your aunt's estate is broken up."

"Only Greta would disagree with you," Steve replied. "In fact, the entire village is up in arms over the situation . . . I guess everyone feels a way of life is being threatened: Old World traditions, neighbors helping neighbors, family members caring for one another . . . old folks, youngsters, newlyweds—"

"Understandable." Rosco interrupted as gently as he could. "You said that she and your uncle Amos had been married for only two years?"

"That's right. He met her down in Philadelphia during one of his infrequent forays into an urban environment. The next thing you knew we had an 'Aunt Greta.' "

Rosco smiled. "You make her sound like an orphaned rattlesnake. It must have been difficult for her to make friends—"

"You can say that again. I don't know anyone who didn't think she was a gold digger as well as a *city slicker*."

"Tell me a little more about your uncle's death," Rosco pushed. "You mentioned it was unexpected."

His response was tinted with a deep tone of devotion. "You remember Amos, don't you, Rosco? The epitome of the Pennsylvania Dutch elder: an ox of a man with a booming voice and a handshake that could crunch bones. He told me one time that when he'd had measles as a kid, his teacher had turned him away from the classroom out of fear he'd infect the other students . . . Those were the only days he missed school . . ." Steve chuckled briefly at the memory. "Absolutely nothing got Amos down. Nothing. Even in his seventies he was out there plowing with his team of mules—on foot, too . . . But then there was a community event—a potluck supper—and Amos contracted food poisoning . . ."

"Did a lot of people get sick?" Rosco asked.

"No . . . Just Uncle Amos."

NIGHT brought a heavy snowfall; and at dawn it was snowing still. The sun tried in vain to put in an appearance, then left the sky colored a thin, winter gray while the fields and distant barns and farmhouses vanished under an ever-growing blanket of white. Bird-in-Hand existed only as a tiny settlement: a main street, a crossroads, a handful of homes, as if in the space of twelve hours, time had flown backward two hundred years.

The sense of remove was strengthened as Rosco entered the kitchen and found Hannah making coffee over the wood stove.

"The electricity's out," she said cheerfully. "Not that it's an unusual occurrence during a storm . . . Lucky thing I made the sticky buns yesterday—"

"And it's a lucky thing Belle and I don't live any closer to you two. You'd have to roll us in and out the door—and then bounce us down the street."

"Nothing wrong with a sticky bun once in a while," was Hannah's breezy response.

"Or a daily helping of shoofly pie . . . or potatoes mashed in cream . . . or lima beans in a cheese sauce . . . sausages in gravy . . . or bread with real butter."

"Don't forget scrapple." Hannah chuckled. "Hey, you want *nouvelle cuisine,* you gotta go to where they do things *nouvelle.*"

"Why does that statement remind me of Steve?"

"I guess most married couples end up sharing a single brain."

"The lucky ones," Steve added as he entered the kitchen. Despite the buoyant words, his expression still wasn't happy.

"It's okay, hon," his wife said. "We'll find a way to keep everything the way Meg wanted it. Cheer up—it's beginning to look a lot like Christmas—"

"Hmmm. This is going to be the first Christmas we won't be celebrating in the Sutter family home. The first holiday Meg will miss."

"I know," was Hannah's quiet reply.

* * *

ROSCO and Steve arrived back at Meg's to find Greta waiting on the porch.

"You didn't lock everything up last night."

"Yes, I believe I—" Steve began, but Greta interrupted with an impatient:

"I don't know why you insist on poking around this old place. Just a lot of musty memories."

"That's not what my aunt Meg felt," Steve answered coolly. "And it's not the opinion of the local folks, either. And speaking of poking around—"

"Well, it's *my* opinion," Greta shot back while pointedly ignoring Rosco. "Just make sure you don't disturb anything—like you did yesterday. The auctioneers have already cataloged the collection, and the moving truck and crew arrive tomorrow afternoon; *if* this damn snow calls it quits in time." Then she stormed off the porch, waded through snow drifts to her car, and attempted to speed off, zigzagging dangerously across the roadway and spewing exhaust in her wake.

"Charming lady," Rosco observed. "Good thing there wasn't a big truck out there."

Steve smiled and raised his eyebrows. "Yeah, that sure is fortunate, all right."

"I didn't realize Greta was so much younger than your uncle."

He gave a terse laugh. "That fact didn't sit well with Meg, I can tell you . . . though she really tried hard to be tolerant. Everyone did. We all wanted—hoped—that Uncle Amos would be happy."

"But you suspected otherwise?"

"Just suspicions, that's all."

As they entered the house, Steve flicked the light switch, but nothing happened. He flicked it twice more before saying, "Oh boy . . . I forgot the power's out. If it stays out much longer, I'll need to light a fire to keep the pipes from bursting. Come on, Aunt Meg kept some candles in the kitchen."

The two men passed through the rooms, and Rosco posed another question. "Did Meg share your feelings that all wasn't perfect in her brother's marriage?"

Steve stopped in his tracks. "Meg couldn't abide Greta. Flat out. Insisted she was sneaky and conniving; a 'heart of a magpie' was a term she used. Of course, she didn't say any of that till Amos was gone . . . But three and a half weeks after his death, Meg mistook Hannah for Greta and screamed to beat the band . . .

even went so far as accusing Hannah of 'villainous threats.' It was a lucky thing I was here and could intervene and calm her down."

Rosco shook his head. "That's gotta be tough."

"We could almost pinpoint Meg's mental decline from that date: reciting the alphabet backward instead of speaking, talking in rhymes . . . Once, she even left the doors open so 'the bees could come in and nest' . . . She could be entirely lucid on occasion, but those times grew increasingly infrequent—especially with *Greedy Greta* lurking around so often."

Rosco stared, somewhat surprised. "Greta had access to the house at the time?"

"Yep. Meg had never locked a door in her life, and the doctor in Lancaster advised us not to alter her habits. Hannah and I tried to monitor Greta's visits, but if we were out of town, attending a craft show—"

Rosco assimilated the information as the two men walked into the kitchen, found the candles, and proceeded back toward the parlor. "Was there a criminal investigation into Amos's cause of death?"

Steve stopped and faced Rosco. "Absolutely not. Folks were upset enough; everyone who'd contributed food to the potluck felt to blame."

"I didn't mean that type of investigation. I'm talking about a basic medical examiner's report: the contents of the deceased's stomach, that sort of thing."

"An autopsy? We've never had a need for that stuff around here," was the somewhat edgy reply.

"Okay." Rosco remained quiet a moment before posing his next question. "Meg's illness . . . the physical manifestations of it . . . Were there any symptoms that seemed similar to your uncle's?"

Steve studied his friend. "Are you . . . are you suggesting Greta might have—?" He didn't finish the thought.

"I don't know what I'm suggesting, Steve . . . But the timing of the two deaths is bothering me—especially given the fact that your aunt and uncle were two apparently healthy and robust people. Accidents happen, sure, I know that. And people coping with grief often decline physically—and rapidly, but . . ."

"But . . . ?"

"That's just it . . . All I have to go on is a hunch we're missing something." Rosco paused. "You're convinced Meg intended to write another will. I'm with you on that, but we need more . . . We need to corroborate your aunt's mistrust of her sister-in-law."

"I don't mind telling any judge what I've just told you."

"I'm afraid that's not good enough. It would only be your word against Greta's . . . You tell the court how your aunt screamed bloody murder when she mistook your wife for her sister-in-law. Greta claims it was Hannah who was at fault. It goes nowhere. In other words, you lose."

"I see your point," Steve admitted after a long minute of silence.

"But what I'm thinking is this . . . Is it possible your aunt might have written something indicating a change of heart . . . '*Intent*' is the proper term . . . For instance, did she keep a diary, maybe start to write a letter that wasn't mailed—even scribble in a cookbook? When older people can't sleep at night, they often jot down notes about things they don't want to forget; then they toss 'em in a drawer and lose track of them. Of course, any indication of a change of heart would need to be dated as well."

"Greta cleaned out everything in Meg's bedroom; and the only letters my aunt ever wrote were to me in college." His expression had grown dark and troubled once more. "As for cookbooks, her recipes were handed down verbally from her mother and great-grandmother . . . Sorry, Rosco, but the only pieces of loose paper in the house are Meg's old crossword puzzles."

"And the *frakturs.*"

Steve allowed himself the smallest of smiles. "I don't care how mentally unsound my aunt was at the end, she *never* would have written on one of her precious *frakturs*."

Rosco nodded. "Then I'd suggest we start looking through the crosswords. Maybe we'll find a phrase, a doodle . . . something that might help us."

Steve stood quietly with his hands in his pockets for a moment. Then he shrugged and said, "What the heck . . . It's worth a shot."

IT took over two hours to collect the hundreds of puzzles Meg Sutter had stashed in dresser drawers, closets, under window seats, in antique baskets, and old wooden apple boxes. When they'd finished, the dining room table was stacked high with bundles of crosswords tied with twine or folded into cardboard boxes. Among them sat the candles, flickering dimly and lending the scene an oddly medieval feel.

"This is interesting," Rosco said as he picked up a candlestick and held it closer to one of the stacks.

"These puzzles all have themes beginning with the letter B: Baseball, The Beatles, Broadway Shows. I guess your aunt arranged her word games alphabetically rather than by newspaper or date."

"This is going to take us months," was Steve's dejected response. "There must be a thousand crosswords here . . . and Meg obviously completed each one."

"We could start with M for Message . . . W for Will?" Rosco offered, but his friend didn't appear to be amused. Instead, the two men began to carefully open every piece of folded newsprint, scanning each section for a potential communication from Meg. "All we need to do is establish intent," Rosco reiterated. "And date."

"I'd rather see the words LOOK UNDER THE HALL CARPET FOR MY NEW WILL," said Steve with a smile.

"You and me both, buddy."

An hour later, Steve found a newspaper that contained an empty puzzle grid and no clues. "Look at this . . . Aunt Meg never attempted this one. In fact, she cut out the clues and only saved the grid."

"Let me see." Rosco took the folded newsprint, and as he did, a piece of paper dropped to the floor. He studied it as he picked it up. Handwritten, in separate columns, were Across and Down clues. Meg Sutter's signature appeared at the bottom. "Your aunt used this published puzzle grid but created her own clues . . . and her own solution . . ."

Steve retrieved a pencil from the kitchen while Rosco began reading clues aloud. "6-Down . . . *Certain flounders* . . . The solution contains eleven letters . . ."

"WINDOW PANES," Steve said. "They were Aunt Meg's favorite fish. She and I used to share a joke about 'cleaning window panes' . . . She didn't like either job." He smiled at the memory. "This is almost like having her write me a letter . . . almost like having her talking to me . . ." He pointed to 9-Across. "*Barcelona buddy* . . . AMIGO! Hah, and you accused me of never studying in Spanish class . . ."

Rosco smiled and wrote, but after another fifteen minutes the men were stopped cold. "I hate to admit this, but we're going to have to call the expert."

"The phone's in the kitchen."

"It's not one of those hand-crank numbers, is it?" Rosco jested.

"You'd be amazed how hard it was to get Aunt Meg to even *consider* Touch-Tone."

"Try me," Rosco said as he lifted the receiver to phone Belle in Massachusetts. He found the line dead, then sighed a half-amused, half-frustrated: "No electricity, no phone . . . Is this a plot?"

"Hey, folks did just fine before the advent of the information superhighway."

"That's a joke, right?" He reached into a zippered pocket in his parka and pulled out his cell phone. "Tah-dah, modern technology saves the day."

By the thin and snowy light filtering through the windows, Rosco continued to peruse clues while waiting for Belle to answer. "Oregon border town?" he asked the moment she picked up. "Five letters, begins with N."

Her reply was a quick chuckle and an indulgent: "NYSSA . . . and hi to you, too . . . Or are we dispensing with the formalities from now on?" Then she added, "What gives? I thought you were helping Steve with an inheritance issue."

"I am . . . I think . . . What about a Washington border town beginning with K and ending with O? Five letters."

"KELSO." Belle laughed. "What are you guys doing: playing Scrabble? No proper names; remember the rules?"

Rosco answered with a rather lame, "It's snowing—"

"It's December. It's *supposed* to snow. We're getting pounded up here, too. A good day to be curled up in front of the fire . . . With someone you love . . . If you get my drift. Pun intended."

"Actually, what happened is that Steve and I found a crossword—"

"And I love you too, Rosco . . . Look, if you wanted to become a word game addict, you could have stayed home . . . In front of the fire, with someone you—"

"No. It belonged to Meg."

"Something tells me I'm not getting through—"

"It's a published puzzle grid to which she added her own words and clues."

A quick intake of breath greeted this information. Rosco could tell that his bride was mentally sitting up and taking notice now. "Let me guess . . . Your theory is that she left a message hidden in the crossword—"

"It sounds loony, I know—"

"No, it doesn't. I remember reading about a case like that in England . . . it was five or six years ago . . . Look, I don't want to cast aspersions on your lexical talents—or on Steve's—but why don't you just fax me the crossword. It'll save time."

"I told you it was snowing—"

"And?"

"And the electricity's off. The phones, too."

Belle groaned, and Rosco laughed.

"Don't say it," she groused.

His response was a not-so-innocent, "Say what?"

" 'Curiosity killed the cat.' " Belle sighed. "Call me as soon as you discover anything . . . Call me for any reason *whatever* . . . Or I could just stay on the line—"

"Not on *my* cell phone bill you don't. Besides, we *are* two grown men, Belle—with *reasonably* developed vocabularies."

She didn't respond to this sally, instead asking a pointed, "I guess you're not willing to supply further info?"

"Not yet . . . All we've got to go on is a hunch and a questionable cause of death."

"But I thought Meg—"

"I'll let you know if I learn anything."

Again, Belle sighed. "I'll be here. I'll be waiting."

"One quick thing before you go—"

"What's that?"

"A five-letter word for *Not right*?"

"Wrong?"

"Hah! Nice try . . . but no way, José. Keep those home fires burning!"

* * *

AN arduous hour later, the crossword was complete. Steve stared at it without speaking, and in that space of time, a single lamp in the kitchen glowed into life, although neither of the friends was aware that the world of electrical current and high-speed communications had soundlessly returned to the Lancaster County hamlet.

"Why do you suppose Meg created this and then hid it?" Steve wondered aloud.

"Could she have been worried about Greta's reaction?" Rosco asked. "Worried about possible consequences? That it would be destroyed out of hand?"

Steve continued to gaze at the crossword. "But Meg and I were so close. She could have—"

"Maybe she believed she *had* shared this with you already. Remember, her mind was playing serious tricks on her."

Steve said nothing while Rosco returned his attention to the crossword. "No month or year . . . no newspaper of origin . . . Even with Meg's own words, there's no way we can contest the will Greta possesses. Like you said, we need a date."

The men sat in discouraged silence until Rosco suddenly reached for his cell phone.

"Just because there's no date left on the newspaper doesn't mean there wasn't one there to begin with." He punched ten numbers into the phone; Belle answered on the first ring.

"No, all we have is a grid and Meg's handwritten clues . . ." Rosco cupped his hand over the phone and turned to Steve. "I was right, Belle thinks she may be able to trace the puzzle by its design. She knows most of the puzzle editors at the major daily newspapers. If we could just get to a fax—"

Simultaneously, both men became aware of the change in light.

"The power's back on . . ." Steve almost shouted. "And yes, I have a fax in my studio . . ."

Rosco raised his eyebrows in a mocking fashion.

"And no, I don't want to hear any quips about the modern age. Remember, I'm a businessman." He had his jacket and gloves on before he stopped speaking.

Rosco bowed facetiously and said, "Please lead on, oh Twenty-First-Century Man."

* * *

IN Steve's woodworking shop, time passed and the fax remained dishearteningly silent. Rosco paced among the tools of Sutter's trade, picking them up and examining them as if they were as strange to him as surgical instruments.

"Jigsaw?" he asked as he placed his hand on the base of one of the few power tools.

"Band saw."

"Right . . . And of course, this would be a . . . a . . . ?"

"Lathe."

"Absolutely. That's what I thought."

Rosco picked up another tool from the workbench, and Steve said, "Coping saw," without waiting for Rosco to ask.

"Huh. No glue gun? Everything in our house is held together with a glue gun. It's my tool of choice. Kind of a Martha Stewart thing . . . I've been thinking of getting a holster for it."

Steve was giving only partial attention to Rosco's banter. "I hope we don't lose power again . . ." he muttered under his breath. "Maybe a tree limb took out another phone line."

Suddenly the fax sprang to life, spitting out Meg's crossword and a lengthy note from Belle. Rosco read it and began paraphrasing for his anxious friend. "The puzzle, i.e. the grid and original clues, was syndicated throughout the country July twenty-third of this year. Bingo, we're dated! That's nineteen days after Amos's death, and almost eighteen months *after* the will Greta has—"

Steve interrupted. "So the end of the message at 42- and 61-Across—"

"No question about it . . . I say they definitely refer to Amos's passing. And Meg's illness, too . . . Looks like your Christmas gift has arrived just in time, my friend."

ACROSS

1. Not right
6. Roll of cash
9. Barcelona buddy
14. Richardson or Fiennes
15. Writer Levin
16. Enticed
17. A Bird in the Hand, 1
20. Stomped on
21. Butterfly snagger
22. Smokehouse specialty
25. Englishmen's sun?
28. Sib of sis
31. "____my word"
33. Distress
34. Watermelon annoyance
35. A Bird in the Hand, 2
40. Fountain treat
41. Set of two
42. A Bird in the Hand, 3
49. Certain milkweed
50. Corn unit
51. Stratagem
52. Consumed
53. Confused
57. Partnership inits.
58. Air; comb form
59. Consumer
61. A Bird in the Hand, 4
69. Ryan or Tatum
70. .001 inch
71. Spell of indulgence
72. Unique individuals
73. Knot
74. Missouri feeder

DOWN

1. Big name at Notre Dame
2. ____de mer
3. Under the weather
4. One way to dispose of 34-Across
5. Clipped
6. Certain flounders
7. Mr. Onassis
8. 28-Across parent
9. Back street
10. Join
11. Ms. Lupino
12. Head of state? abbr.
13. Little bill
18. Seek affection
19. Three____match
22. Hovel
23. Mil. address
24. 28-Across parent
26. Drama from 37-Down
27. Tough place to crawl out of?
28. Wax maker
29. Gun
30. Lyric poem
32. Oregon border town
34. Remove paint
36. Tip the noggin
37. Tokyo, formerly
38. Rogue
39. Letter opener?
42. "Found it!"
43. Home site
44. Affirmative vote

A Partridge in a Pear Tree

1	2	3	4	5	■	6	7	8	■	9	10	11	12	13
14					■	15			■	16				
17					18				19					
■	■	■	20				■	■	21			■	■	■
22	23	24	■	25			26	27			■	28	29	30
31			32	■	■	33			■	■	34			
35				36	37				38	39				
■	■	■	40				■	41				■	■	■
42	43	44					45					46	47	48
49				■	■	50			■	■	51			
52			■	53	54				55	56	■	57		
■	■	■	58			■	■	59			60	■	■	■
61	62	63				64	65					66	67	68
69					■	70			■	71				
72					■	73			■	74				

45. Treat for Trigger
46. Building addition
47. Storage tub
48. Stop
53. Breakfast, lunch, and dinner
54. NYC subway line
55. Sugar; suffix
56. Washington border town
58. A ways off
60. Tears
61. Also
62. Rest stop
63. Catch sight of
64. Rescue pro
65. Jr.'s son
66. Time of note
67. Broc. or spin.
68. Shoe size

Mum's the Word

ACROSS

1. Grudge
5. 1-Across, e.g.
9. Ploy
11. Criticize
13. With 4-Down, New Year's Day
14. Philly's strutters
16. Antique
17. Pitch
19. Merida Mrs.
20. Quaker foe?
21. Saunters
23. Poker pile
24. "_____ luck!"
26. Web address; abbr.
27. Drudgery
29. Herman and Allen
31. Hightails
33. Alien craft; abbr.
34. Some hosp. rooms
35. Odd-ball
38. "_____ in St. Louis"
41. Behind the _____ ball
42. A Gardner
44. Bloodier
46. NBC offering
47. Breathes their last
50. Retirement acct.
51. Here, in Italy
52. Stinks
53. Russian fighter
54. A-One
57. Jail bird
60. Compositions
61. TV show opener
62. Some msgs.
63. H. H. Munro

DOWN

1. Not so honest hombre
2. Old French coin
3. Flight info
4. See 13-Across
5. Schuylkill sight
6. Actress Dawber
7. Cash mach.
8. "X Marks _____"
9. 37-Down ingredient
10. Island off Turkey
11. Like 52-Across
12. "The Comedy of _____"
13. Actor Grey
15. Quench
18. Super ending?
21. Untimely demise?
22. Plate passers?
25. Bridge position
28. Certain perennial
30. Hither and _____
32. Runner Sebastian
35. Revolutionary man?
36. Least attractive
37. Candles
38. In Europe it's common
39. Pyramid architect, formally
40. Odder
41. Some lwyrs.
43. Strive
45. Fad
48. Takes a look inside?
49. Road turns
55. WWII craft
56. Set down
58. FAA predecessor
59. Question

Mum's the Word

NAH, nah, the first Freddie Five Fingers was killed back in 'Fifty-four at Fifth and Fitzwater on February fourteenth . . . Way before my time, obviously, but sort of Philadelphia's version of the Saint Valentine's Day Massacre . . . Of course, Freddie was the only goon bumped off, so *massacre*'s kind of a stretch of the imagination, even by South Philly standards."

Jack Keegan stabbed his fork into his one remaining gingered shrimp and popped it into his mouth. Although he'd eaten lunch in Chinatown—Noh Joy's, to be precise—twice a week for the last thirty years, he still had yet to warm up to the idea of chopsticks. "My hands are like potatoes here," he was fond of saying. "I trip over my own fingers. I mean, look at these mitts." Then he'd flex his broad hands, emphasizing their size and strength—the necessary tools of the trade when one's trade was mixing it up with underworld characters on a daily basis.

Jack Keegan had spent his entire FBI career chasing down mobsters in South Philadelphia. Up until now, it had been a more or less break-even situation, or as he liked to say: "Sometimes you get the bear, sometimes the bear gets you." Lately, however, law enforcement had been on the winning side. A number of high-ranking, high-profile hoods had been convicted of an assortment of crimes and dispatched to a *tight* facility in Western Pennsylvania, resulting in a marked slowdown in nefarious activity south of South Street.

"Since the summer things have been—"

Jack was interrupted as Belle Graham abruptly sneezed. In unison, he and Rosco said, "God bless you."

"Thanks. I hope I'm not coming down with something—" She sneezed again, pulled a tissue from her pocket, and dabbed at her nose. "I had no idea Philadelphia had such a colorful history—other than the Declaration of Independence, Liberty Bell, Constitution, et cetera, which are obviously no slouches in terms of national significance . . . But the Mummers Parade . . . Would you say it's like Mardi Gras in New Orleans, except cold?"

"Cold. Right . . ." Jack nodded. "Anyway, I was gonna say that things were pretty quiet around here until Christmas Day. That's when Freddie Five Fingers—the *second* Freddie Five Fingers, that is—turned up dead."

"Not to be flip," Rosco interjected, "but doesn't everyone have five fingers?"

"Yeah, right . . . but *this* Freddie's real name was Hermann, so he just adopted the name from the *first* Freddie, hoping the slimy lowlife reputation would follow. It has a better ring than, say, Horse Head Hermann; at least in South Philly . . . Then, over the years he kind of lost the *Fingers* part, and was basically just known as Freddie Five."

Rosco shrugged, unsure if his question about the five fingers had been answered or not.

"And Freddie was a bookmaker?" Belle asked through a sniffle, using her cup of green tea to warm her hands.

"Ostensibly. He was real good with numbers, real good. But Freddie Five was into just about everything—none of the rough stuff, though. Never a hit or knee capping."

"And you never knew it was Freddie Five who was secretly sending you those, ah . . . *instructive* crossword puzzles?" Rosco asked.

"Well, they never went directly to the FBI; they were always submitted to the local newspaper, the *Philadelphia Inquirer*—known hereabouts as the 'Inky' . . . When Freddie's first puzzle arrived—this was about four years ago—one of the editors got suspicious and forwarded it to us. The messages were always fairly obvious; DRUG DEAL ON NINTH—" Jack looked at Belle with a proud smile. "Fifteen letters, right? Fits right across a daily puzzle grid, huh?"

She nodded and sniffled once again.

"Yeah, I remember that one . . . Anyway, Freddie'd do something like: CORNER OF KIMBALL, BE THERE AT FOUR AM, LOOK FOR JOEY DOGS; that sort of thing. He was real good . . . I mean, the things looked like the genuine article . . . Actually, they were the genuine article . . . Like this one I gave you. Which is why he never blew his cover . . . So as

I was sayin', these crossword tip-offs would appear every six months or so. The editor would send them to the Bureau, and we'd move in and make the bust. But we never knew it was Freddie Five who constructed them. Never would have figured he was a snitch. Freddie was a real high-profile guy—"

"Until he turned up dead."

"Right. That's when we found that puzzle in a kitchen drawer." Keegan pointed at the *Mum's the Word* crossword. "We realized that Freddie Five had been our informant all this time. The handwriting's a dead ringer—if you will—for the other puzzles. But for the life of me, we can't make hide nor hair of this one."

"It has a nice symmetry," Belle agreed, "but you're right, there's nothing foreboding about these answers—just a slight New Year's Day theme."

"I sure appreciate the two of you making the trip down from Massachusetts to help out with this. Like I said before, your reputations precede you. And I figured if anyone could get into Freddie Five's word-game psyche, it would be Belle. I'm guessing he wouldn't have made that puzzle unless he was trying to tip us off to something. Something big."

It was Rosco who posed the next question. "I'm assuming you believe his associates had uncovered his double life?"

"I'm certain of it. It was a classic mob hit: .22 right behind the ear. But I don't think they knew *how* Freddie was passing the skinny to us, or they wouldn't have left this piece of evidence behind. His place was torn apart." Jack split open his fortune cookie and groaned. " 'All things come to he who waits.' What the hell is this?" He turned and looked toward the kitchen. "I think Noh Joy sets me up with these cookies . . . She sees me coming. She likes to torment me. She knows I'm not a patient kind of guy."

Rosco reached for his own cookie. "But I don't see why Freddie would snitch on his own people . . . What was in it for him? Clearly, he wasn't on the Bureau's payroll."

"No way. But every goon he ratted on was into him for five or six large ones, and—"

"Large ones?" Belle interrupted.

"Large ones. A grand . . . thousand dollars. Each of these guys Freddie fingered owed him over five thousand dollars in gambling losses . . . Sometimes, a whole lot more . . . And these musclemen are notorious for sticking bookies with their losses. They're the first ones at the door when the Eagles beat the point-spread, but they're nowhere to be found when it comes time to collect the damage . . . Guys like Freddie just have to write it off as bad debt—protection money, if you will. You push 'em for the coin, you wind up in Pennsylvania Hospital."

"But Freddie found a way of getting even," Belle mused.

"You got it . . .'til it all caught up with him."

Rosco opened his cookie. " 'Dance and the whole world dances favorably' . . . Must have lost something in the translation." He shrugged and tossed the slip of paper into the ashtray. "Any idea who might have killed your man?"

"I'd bet money it was ordered by Nicky Grapes, but he probably wasn't the trigger man. He seems to be the one most likely to step into Sonny Pancakes's shoes since Sonny got sent up last summer."

"These are real names—Pancakes, Grapes?" Belle asked.

"Nah. All these guys have street names. Like Sonny never got any sun? Never went 'down the shore,' as they say. He was always white as batter . . . So they called him Pancakes."

"And Grapes?"

"Grapes. You know, it's slang for . . ." Jack cleared his throat and looked at Rosco for help.

Rosco said, "Eh . . . I think it might have something to do with wine consumption."

"Hmmm," Belle said, sneezed once more, and read off her fortune. " 'Seek and you shall find the truth.' I like that. I guess I should be studying this crossword a little closer . . ."

"Freddie was always very clear on the: *WHO, WHAT, WHERE*, and *WHEN* clues . . . But I'm not seeing those in this puzzle." Keegan made no attempt to hide his frustration.

"Well, we do have JANUARY FIRST as the solution to 13-Across and 4-Down. And MUMMERS at 14-Across. That's a start."

"Along with the title," Rosco added as he looked at Agent Keegan. "It looks to me like you're right in suspecting that something might be going down at the Mummers Parade tomorrow."

Jack groaned again. "That's what I kept coming up with. Freddie's got MARKET at 38-down . . . That's the main street for the parade route. Center City. What a nightmare. Have you two ever been to the Mummers Parade?"

"I saw some of it on TV when I was young," Belle said. "It looked like fun."

"Unless you're trying to look for someone—or something. Every person marching is a member of a club—a real old tradition: one hundred years plus, and still going strong . . . Quaker City's one of the more famous groups, prize winners, too; Irish American's another club; then there's Ferko, Satin Slippers, Hog Island, 2nd Street Shooters—"

"2nd Street Shooters?" Rosco asked. "Wouldn't that be a logical place to start searching for your alleged killer?"

Keegan chortled although the sound was less than cheery. "It's just a name, Rosco . . . like Hog Island, which was the location of the largest shipbuilding enterprise during World War One; 'Hog Islanders,' they called themselves . . . Anyway, the clubs are divided into Fancy Brigades, Comic Divisions, and String Bands. Some have real elaborate floats, maybe entire production numbers with sets that split apart . . . and every participant is gussied up in sequins and feathers—the gaudier the getup, the better—with masks or painted faces. You wouldn't recognize your own brother if he came up and spat on you."

"So you've got your *WHERE* and *WHEN,* albeit fairly vague." Belle's tone was pensive. "Maybe if we can determine the *WHO* and *WHAT*, we could narrow things down a little."

"Right, but remember we're talking about two *WHO*s here—the perp and the mark—and we can't ID either one."

"You mentioned the man who liked Grapes?" Belle said.

"Uhh . . . Right . . . But there's another possibility." Keegan pointed to the puzzle. "57-Across, ESCAPEE. We had a guy break out of a medium-security joint up in Sesquichi about a month ago—Tony Starch."

"Because of his shirts?" Belle asked.

"Huh?"

"Because he liked extra starch in his shirts? That's how he got the nickname?"

"Oh . . . I see. No, no, *Starch* is his real name. His street name is . . . Well, it used to be Tony November, but he now goes by Tony Scorps. That's why I use his real name. It gets confusing after a while."

"Oh, I get it . . ." Belle answered. "November, because he was born in that month, and Scorps, because he's a Scorpio."

"Not bad . . . You're definitely getting the hang of it. He's even got a scorpion tattooed on the back of each hand."

Belle sneezed for what seemed like the hundredth time. Rosco put his arm around her shoulders. "You sound terrible. I think we'd better get you back to the hotel. I'm afraid your tour of the City of Brotherly Love is going to have to come out of the guidebook."

She leaned into Rosco's shoulder. "You're probably right . . ." Then she looked at Jack Keegan. "I'm sorry I couldn't be more help. Where do you go from here?"

"As much as I hate to say it, this Mummers thing is all we have to go on. Some of the brigades are rehearsing at the Convention Center. I know a few guys, inside guys . . . I'll see if anything fishy's going on."

"Mind if I tag along?" Rosco asked.

"Be my guest. I need all the help I can get . . . And, Belle, you keep the crossword. You never know. You might get a flash of inspiration. Save us all a heck of a lot of trouble if you did."

Instead of responding, Belle sneezed again.

THE Philadelphia Convention Center was much like other big-city convention facilities, with one major exception: a portion of the building had once served as the grand terminus of the Reading Railroad; and the classic nineteenth-century architecture had been artfully incorporated into a newer, even more expansive structure that gleamed with strategically placed laser and neon lights and long, sleek surfaces of stainless steel and marble. Modern multicolored sculptural installations dangled from the ceiling, appearing to defy gravity. Philadelphia past and present, the hub of nineteenth-century commerce boldly embracing the twenty-first.

"This is really something," Rosco said as he and Jack Keegan stepped off the escalator that had brought them up from street level.

"Yeah, they were going to tear Reading Terminal down before someone got the bright idea to save it. Back in the old days trains used to bring in the produce from Lancaster County. The original marketplace is still right below us." He pointed at his feet. "Hasn't changed a lick in a hundred years. Fruit and vegetable merchants, poultry and egg vendors, fishmongers, and the best French and Italian cheeses north of the Italian Market on Christian Street. My grandad had a butcher stall . . . Hell, I damn near grew up in this building. Woulda been a real tragedy to have lost it. You want real Philly-style food: porchétta and pepper sandwiches, scrapple, cheesesteak. You come here."

A tall, thin man in a red sweatshirt with TEMPLE LAW stitched on the front approached, and extended his hand to the FBI agent.

"Yo, Jack, what's shakin'? Come to watch us strut our stuff?"

Keegan shook his hand. "Just the man I'm looking for. Pete Dixon, meet Rosco Polycrates. Rosco's down from Massachusetts."

"Pleasure," Pete said, assuming Rosco was another FBI agent.

"Dixon was the lead prosecutor at Sonny Pancakes's trial," Keegan explained. "He also happens to be the captain of one of the best string bands around."

"So you're marching in tomorrow's parade?" Rosco asked.

"Wouldn't miss it for the world. Quaker City has won the competition four years running. That's got to be adjusted. This is our year. I feel it in my bones." There was a smile on Dixon's face, but there was no mistaking that he and his club were out to win.

"You heard about Freddie Five?" Jack said, getting right to business.

"Yo? Who hasn't?"

"It turns out Freddie was our crossword snitch, and we've got a strong indication that there's going to be some *discord* at tomorrow's parade."

"And you're thinking it may come my way?"

Jack only shrugged, so Pete Dixon continued:

"Well, if someone's aiming to get even for Sonny Pancakes, your troubles are just beginning. I know of two witnesses who are marching in the Comic Division; three guys from my office alone are in the Fancy Brigades, two more in another string band; and I'll bet you'll find half the damn jurors out there somewhere too . . . Not to mention the arresting officers—like you."

"And Tony Starch broke out a month ago. You heard that?"

"Yo?" Pete Dixon said it with a distinct *Whaddya-think? I was born yesterday?* inflection. "He was into Freddie big time . . ." Then he let out a hearty laugh. "Looks like you got your hands full, Agent Keegan."

Jack ignored the ribbing. "I was hoping you could be a little more helpful than that. Anybody you know having troubles with the mob? Anybody talking? Acting strange? Up to their ears in debt?"

"Come on, Jack, I'm with the DA's office. Nobody says boo around me. Even my mother won't tell me who her bookie is."

"I don't suppose you'd consider sitting out the parade this year?"

Dixon looked at him sideways and said, "Yo?" The meaning of the word this time was, *Whaddya-nuts?*

"I didn't think so."

"Look, Jack, if you're right about a hit taking place tomorrow, I wouldn't waste your time worrying about me. These guys don't whack DAs—they whack each other, especially suspected snitches." He patted his sweatshirt as though he were looking for something. "You got a piece of paper?"

Rosco produced a small pad and a pen from his jacket and handed them to Dixon. Dixon spoke as he wrote:

"And I wouldn't worry too much about Tony Starch either. He's a second-story man. Probably in California by now—if he's smart. Although knowing Tony . . ." Dixon shook his head, then ripped a sheet of paper from the pad, handed it to Keegan, and returned the pen and pad to Rosco. "Those are the names of the two guys who turned state's evidence against Sonny Pancakes. They're both marching in the Comic Division tomorrow; they're with the Fin-n-Feather Club, though I don't know how anyone would recognize them—not with all the makeup and wigs."

"But the flip side is that a hit man could be walking right next to them, and they wouldn't know it."

"You got that right, Keegan."

IT was almost 11 P.M. when Rosco arrived back at the hotel. He and Belle stayed in the room and ordered up a late dinner from room service. To bring in the New Year, he had a T-bone steak, she a large bowl of chicken broth. They sat at a small table near the window, overlooking the massive pillars of the Second Bank of the United States on Chestnut Street. Belle kept a box of tissues by her side at all times. It wasn't the most romantic of meals.

"I'm really sorry, Rosco," she said between spoonfuls of soup and sniffles. "This isn't a great New Year's Eve, but the concierge said there's a terrific fireworks display down by the Delaware River at midnight." She glanced at her watch. "Fifteen minutes. It's only five blocks from here . . . Why don't you go without me?"

"I don't think so. I say we just cozy down in bed and watch the entire thing on TV."

"That bed is huge. I felt like I was napping on a football field this afternoon."

"It's obviously been designed for recreational activity."

"Hmmm. That's not a bad idea . . ." Belle grinned as she finished her soup. "So, what's the story with the state's witnesses the DA told you about?"

"Well, they seemed genuinely nervous—"

"Are they backing out of the parade?"

"No. They told Keegan that Nicky Grapes knows exactly where they live and can get them anytime. Apparently their testimony wasn't so critical that they were placed in the Witness Protection Program."

"Sure, but the costumes and masks would make it impossible for anyone to identify the murderer."

"Jack pointed that out, but the parade's such a big deal for these guys that nobody's going to make them miss it. They asked for extra protection, though."

"And Keegan's going to supply it?"

"He's the one who called them in. He's got to."

Belle pushed her bowl aside and stood. "I'm feeling really crummy. I'm going to get into bed." She crossed the room, removed her robe, slid under the covers, then lifted the photocopy of Freddie's puzzle and began studying it afresh. "*Mum's the Word* . . . There has to be more to this. I must be missing something."

Rosco popped his last French fry into his mouth, finished his glass of wine, doffed his clothes, and slid in beside Belle.

"Did any of these names mean anything to Jack or the DA?" Belle asked as she stared at the puzzle. "WOODY? JOEL? IRA?"

"We scanned the entire list of marchers. Every person in the parade needs to be registered with a group. There were three Iras and seven Joels . . . No Woodys—unless you consider the nicknames of the clarinet players. Keegan contacted everyone he could think of. None admitted any mob connections."

Belle continued to focus on the puzzle. "What about a woman? I see PAM and AVA here."

"It seems that not too many women participate in the parade, but Jack checked those names out too. Three Pams . . . No Avas."

"You know, I keep coming back to this business at 8-Down: 'X *marks* THE SPOT.' Don't you think that should mean something?"

Rosco leaned into her to get a closer look at the crossword. Their bodies were now touching from head to toe. "This is kind of nice," he said. "Too bad you're so sick."

"I'm not all *that* sick." She placed the crossword on the nightstand.

He kissed her neck. "So much for Keegan and Dixon."

"Who's Dixon?"

"The DA . . . Pete Dixon. The guy I've been talking about; the guy who prosecuted Sonny Pancakes."

Belle sat bolt upright. "You never told me his name was Dixon."

"So?"

"So? What's the middle letter in his name?"

"X?"

Rosco jumped out of bed, yanked Jack Keegan's business card out of his jacket, and punched his cell phone number into the telephone. It was the stroke of midnight and the agent had gone to the riverfront to watch the fireworks.

"What are you doing down there?" Rosco asked.

"What?" The explosions were so extreme, he could barely hear a word Rosco was saying.

"I expected you to be at home," Rosco shouted into the phone.

"I find the noise relaxing . . . like the pistol range."

"Listen . . . 'X *marks* THE SPOT!' 'X *marks* THE SPOT'! Dixon has an X in his name. It's Dixon they're after."

Keegan was quiet for a moment. Rosco wasn't sure

if the agent had heard the warning, or was considering a plan of action. Eventually he said, "Sure . . . Sure, that's got to be it."

"Now all you need is the *WHEN*."

"I think that one's obvious . . . I'll suit up in a costume too, and walk the route with Pete . . . Get other available personnel out there . . . We'll be ready for this character no matter when he makes his move."

"Do you need me?"

"No. We can cover it. Besides, something tells me you might not be all that keen about putting on a satin dress and strutting down Market Street with a parasol pretending to be a wench—"

"A what?"

"You heard right . . . another part of the tradition. Someone told me it started in Elizabethan England . . . guys in frilly party dresses and blond braids. Let me tell ya, it makes quite a sight in the men's room . . . Now, get some sleep, Rosco. Watch the Mummers on TV . . . Tell Belle to feel better. And thanks . . ."

"Mummers . . ." Belle murmured as they turned out the light. "Mummery . . . mum . . . keep silent . . ."

* * *

NEW Year's Day Belle and Rosco slept late. They ordered a huge breakfast from room service—waffles, bacon, coffee, grapefruit, and Pennsylvania Dutch sticky buns. Belle's appetite seemed to have returned miraculously, although her voice had become gravelly and deep, making her sound like a cross between Walter Cronkite and Kermit the Frog. When they had finished eating, Rosco left for the lobby to buy a newspaper and Belle picked up her guidebook and slid back into bed.

When Rosco returned and finished with the paper, he picked up the TV remote. "Do you want to watch the parade or the NFL playoff game?"

"Are you serious?"

"Kind of . . ."

"You're not going to watch a football game—not when there's an assassin loose in the city . . ." Belle's tone was incredulous.

"Does it matter that it's the Patriots? And we're shooting for two in a row?"

"Rosco!?"

He pushed the remote. "I guess it's the parade."

"You're darn right."

Rosco located the schedule of marchers in the newspaper. "Well, we missed the entire Comic Division by sleeping so late. I assume nothing earth-shattering happened or the newscasters would be saying something about it. The String Bands come next . . ." Rosco moved his eyes down the paper. "Jeeze, there's eighteen of them. This parade must go on for hours."

"Where does Pete Dixon's group fit in?"

"Let's see . . . They're positioned at number six. But there's no telling where this guy's going to make his move . . . The brigades stop in front of the judging stand near City Hall, perform a routine, and move on. Conceivably, the entire route's one big danger zone."

Rosco dropped the newspaper onto the floor and stared up at the television screen. "Wow, look at these costumes. This really is a spectacle."

"Better than football?" was Belle's facetious reply as she moved her focus from the guidebook to the screen. "Look at the feathers on that one . . . ostrich plumes dyed turquoise and gold . . . and those sequined wings . . . That outfit must weigh a hundred pounds . . . I'm sorry I'm feeling so rotten; it would be nice to be watching all of this in person. Not to mention seeing a little of the city, rather than reading about it . . ."

"Hey, at least you're getting educated . . . And working your appetite back up to snuff."

"Don't talk . . . You handled yourself pretty darn well with those sticky buns . . . Chunko."

"At least I don't sound like a frog." He patted his stomach. "I'm going to have to get a run in this afternoon."

Belle chuckled and glanced back at her guidebook and the foldout map of the city. "It says here that William Penn's objective in founding his colony was to create a place where people of all faiths could worship freely and openly. That's why the Continental Congress convened here; the other colonies still practiced religious intolerance—even persecution . . . I guess that's why we saw so many church spires when we drove in . . . Am I boring you?"

"No, no, go on . . . But take a look at these String Bands. They're really good."

Belle took a quick peek at the TV, then returned to her book. "Penn called the city his 'Greene Countrie Towne'; his design incorporated parks still extant to this day: a central greensward—where City Hall now stands—and four other open areas equally spaced from the center . . . he liked symmetry—"

Rosco laughed. "You mean, kind of like a crossword?"

"Hmmm. Yes, now that you mention it." She reached over to the nightstand, picked up the puzzle, and held it next to the map of center city.

Rosco was fixated on the parade. "Look at the performance these folks are putting on . . . a fire-breathing dragon rising out of a mountain!"

But Belle didn't seem to hear him as she studied the crossword, muttering aloud while she worked. "What if this represents a map of the city? The central black cross being City Hall . . . and these other four shaded areas indicating the parks: Rittenhouse Square, Logan Circle, Franklin Square, and Washington Square . . ."

Rosco looked away from the television screen for the first time. "What are you mumbling about, Kermit?"

"Come over here and look at this."

He joined her on the bed.

"Okay," she said, pointing at the puzzle, "look at this: here we have City Hall; and there's MARKET at 38-Down—"

"But the clue reads: *In Europe it's common—*"

"I know. Indulge me. I realize I may be barking up the wrong tree—"

"With a voice like that? Bark away."

"Rosco!"

"Sorry . . . Go on . . . I'm with you: MARKET at 38-Down—"

"SOUTH is here, at 25-Down—"

"For SOUTH Street? What about CYPRUS at 10-Down? I think I saw that on a street sign yesterday."

"No. That's Cypress Street—like the tree, not the island. That's another thing the guidebook explains: the east-west streets named after trees . . . So, we can't count CYPRUS . . . But what if the EIGHT at 41-Across represents Eighth Street . . . It fits perfectly with the map."

"And if we hang on to our '*X marks* THE SPOT' theory, the only X in the puzzle is right here." Rosco pointed to the X in XRAYS at 48-Down. "And that's nowhere near the Parade route. It would be closer to Seventh and Sansom Streets . . . Does the book indicate what's at that location?"

Belle flipped pages until she found a stylized city map displaying the various sections of the city, and what each was noted for. "Okay . . . Antiques Row . . . The Italian Market . . . Chinatown . . . Penn's Landing . . . Independence Mall . . . Here! Here it is! Seventh and Sansom—Jewelers' Row."

Rosco pointed to 1-Down. "BANDITO . . . ESCAPEE . . . Tony Starch, the second-story man . . .

The guy's going to knock off a jewelry store while the entire city—and police force—are focused on the Mummers Parade."

"But which store? I'll bet there are thirty or forty."

Rosco reached under the nightstand and pulled out the yellow pages. "Okay, we're looking for an address in the seven hundred block of Sansom Street, right?"

Belle nodded.

"Jewelers, jewelers, jewelers," Rosco murmured as he flipped through the phone book. "This isn't too bad; there are only a couple of pages of listings . . . Nope, nothing rings a bell." He flipped the page. "There's a ton of them on Sansom Street . . . A lot on Eighth Street too—"

Belle was peering over his shoulder. "37-Down; the answer to the clue is TAPERS." She pointed. "Taper's Diamond Exchange—"

"That's got to be the place."

"It's at 741 Sansom Street, Suite 308. Obviously it's not a storefront. It must be on the third floor; probably a wholesaler. A wholesaler with a lot of valuable stones."

Rosco jumped off the bed and grabbed his jacket. "Call Keegan on his cell phone. Tell him I'm on my way to Sansom Street."

"Maybe you should wait for the police? This sounds a little dangerous."

He bent down and gave her a kiss. "Don't worry. If this is like any other jewelry section, of any other city, a beat cop is stationed there twenty-four/seven. I'll find him before I do anything stupid."

"It's the 'do anything stupid' part that worries me."

He smiled, said, "I love you. Call Keegan," and charged out the door.

ROSCO covered the four blocks to Jewelers' Row in three minutes. Being a jogger, he wasn't close to being winded. Sansom Street was deserted, every shop closed up tighter than a drum. There were no window shoppers, no casual strollers, no one scurrying about: everyone was at the parade. Even the beat cop Rosco had anticipated encountering was nowhere in sight.

"Okay," he muttered, "741 . . . Has to be on the north side . . ." Rosco seldom carried a gun and he was beginning to question the wisdom of this decision. He started going west, but suddenly saw a glass-paneled door swing open halfway down the block. The number 741, etched in gold leaf, reflected the sunlight. A short man, dressed in a three-piece suit and overcoat, and carrying an attaché case, stepped from the doorway.

"Yo!" Rosco called out. "Tony Scorps!"

The man froze in his tracks and turned slowly, making eye contact with Rosco, before dodging off in the opposite direction. Rosco sprinted after him.

As the two approached Eighth Street, the much-sought-after beat cop rounded the corner, well bundled against the cold and bearing a take-out container of coffee, which splattered on the sidewalk as Tony barreled into him. Rosco shouted out the thief's identity—as well as his own; the cop drew his pistol while Tony Starch snarled out an oath and leaped backward, clutching the case against his chest.

"Put the case down," ordered the cop. His grip tightened on the pistol. "Now!"

Outnumbered, the thief complied—all the time swearing mightily.

The cop simply looked on in silence, then picked up the case and trained his weapon on Rosco and Tony. "Couldn't have done it without ya, Ton'," he said as he began edging his way up the street, leaving Rosco and Tony Starch standing with their hands held high. The officer was halfway around the corner when Keegan and several other FBI agents appeared behind him.

"Bobby Bananas," Keegan said with a smile. "Or is it just plain Bobby B. now? When did you blow back into Philly? Impersonating an officer, too . . . nice touch. It'll look even nicer beside your charge of murder one—"

"Hold on, Keegan. I didn't whack Freddie Five—"

"Oh yeah? Then how did you know Tony was pulling this job?"

Bobby's shoulders sagged. "I ain't sayin' nothin' 'til I talk to my lawyer—"

"Uh-huh . . . 'All things come to he who waits,' Bobby boy."

A Ghost of Christmas Past

THEN she disappeared . . . without a trace. The authorities had bloodhounds searching the grounds and village—both Upper and Lower Slaughter. In fact, the surrounding Cotswolds countryside remained under scrutiny for years. Many of the old-timers said they half expected to find her body while digging for turnips in their gardens—"

"Angus!"

"I'm merely citing sources, Judy."

"That's 'professor-speak' for quoting unabashed raconteurs and gossips, Belle." Judith, round and homespun as a sparrow, gazed fondly at her tall and angular husband, then returned to the all-important preparation of dinner for their newly arrived American guests: the task at hand being to dust a layer of grated Parmesan over a terrine of leeks and potatoes covered with an herb-flecked béchamel sauce.

"And that, *madame et monsieur,*" Angus announced as he pointed to the casserole, "is what happens when a Brit like me gets hitched to a Yank. The lowly leek and spud pie goes Continental."

" 'Continental'?" Judith teased. "Aren't you confusing your geography a wee bit? Or are you referring to the continent of North America?"

"Well, you know what I mean. Cooking becomes 'cuisine' . . . à la Brillat-Savarin and all those fancy culinary blokes—"

"Brillat-Savarin's long gone," his wife laughed. "Nowadays, you need to know the difference between Asian-fusian and—"

"Feta focaccia," her husband added.

"Not *precisely* the analogy I would have drawn."

Angus ignored his wife's gibe, instead raising a garnet-colored glass of port. "Cheers! Here's to Belle Graham, crossword editor, 'egghead,' and valued chum, and here's to our *newest* crony, Rosco, i.e. the doting mister—"

"I don't know about 'doting,' " Belle rejoined.

"All right then: austere, reticent, cantankerous, contentious—"

"How about just plain old, nice guy?" Rosco chuckled as he returned to the previous topic: the peculiar history of their hosts' home. "What happened to Katlin's husband, Richard—after she vanished?"

Judith answered as she placed the terrine in the oven. "There were rumors that she'd been unfaithful . . . A gardener named Tom was mentioned . . . Nothing proven, of course."

Angus joined his wife's recitation. "He was reputed to be a bit of a rum fellow—"

"That's an 'odd duck' to us Yanks." Judith walked to an antique trestle table as she spoke, and began setting places for dinner. Belle joined her, folding napkins and aligning forks and spoons and knives. The two women worked in such silent harmony they might as well have been back in the dorm during their college days—roommates focused on a single task. "What an odd story," Belle finally said. "Unsettling, too . . ."

"All these Cotswolds houses have strange tales attached to them," Judith offered. "It comes with the territory. If a place is four or five hundred years old, it's bound to have witnessed its share of troubling events."

"Take Minster Lovell Hall," added Angus. "A ghost of a place now . . . and probably for good reason—"

"Don't tell that awful 'Mistletoe Bough' story, Angus. You'll be scaring Belle and Rosco half to death."

But Angus, a born tale-teller, was not to be stopped. "Picture this . . . Christmas Eve . . . Let us say three hundred years ago, or four, or even five . . . Around here, the dates are haphazard at best when most folks—and I don't mean solely peers of the realm—are the twelfth or thirteenth in a family line . . .

"So, Christmas Eve with all the attendant hoopla: wassail and song, a home bursting at the seams with visitors, a pig roasting slowly on a spit, minions scurrying about mulling wine and cider . . . and a little girl vanishes while playing hide-and-seek: 'sardines' or 'squashed sardines' being the names of the variants I played as a kid . . . At any rate, the wee person in question creeps on tiptoe through the ancient manse, her velvet gown rustling across the floor, her stiff lace collar clasping a small throat that scarcely dares draw breath so pleased is she to be allowed to play a game with her elder siblings and cousins—"

"Angus! This is circumstantial."

He raised a hand requesting silence. "Children are children the world and intervening ages over . . . I daresay you and Belle would have behaved exactly as the girl in my story."

Judith sighed but it was the indulgent sound of a woman in love with her husband.

"At length, our festively bedecked young lass finds an ideal place of concealment: an aged and unused oaken chest, cobwebby and rusty-hinged. She struggles to raise the lid, choking back her apprehension at the utter darkness inside, then looks about. No one appears to question her actions or give her hiding place away. So without a sound, she sequesters herself within—never to stir again."

Belle gasped. Judith said, "Angus. No more. Please."

But he continued. "The little girl's body was found many, many years later—a small skeleton in the cask in which she'd hidden herself—"

"Wouldn't her parents have turned the place upside down searching for her?" Belle interrupted with some heat.

Angus shrugged. "The answer, I'm afraid, is lost in the centuries. Perhaps, all and sundry hunted in the wrong places: out of doors, or in the cellars, or servants' quarters . . . I would imagine—and this is purely conjecture, mind you—that the searchers would have assumed she would be able to hear them and cry out . . ." He shook his head, leaving the rest of the grim prognosis unspoken. "Then there was also the death of Francis Lovell—"

"Angus, stop!"

"No, I'm interested," said Rosco.

"Ah, the lugubrious brain of an ex-copper," Angus chortled. "Now, that particular Lovell was a supporter of Lambert Simnel . . . You Yanks probably haven't heard tell of him, but he was a rather well-known fifteenth-century impostor—and pretender to the throne. A bloke with a questionable past, as they say, who'd been born the son of a tradesman in Oxford, not too far from here as you know . . . Young Simnel came to the attention of a politically minded priest who decided the handsome youth would do well impersonating a dead prince—rumor being that said royal was *not* demised—"

"Angus!"

He beamed benignly. "My wife doesn't appreciate scholarly digressions . . . At any rate, following a bloody uprising in which the Royalist forces of King

Henry VII won the field, Francis Lovell disappeared, then clandestinely returned to his ancestral home, ensconcing himself in a secret room in order to avoid being arrested as a traitor . . . However, he concealed himself so successfully that he couldn't escape his own prison and so died of starvation."

"How awful," Belle murmured.

"So you see why the history of our tidy home is decidedly staid."

"What do you mean by saying Tom was a 'rum fellow'?" Rosco asked after a moment's pause.

"Gypsy eyes," was Angus's ready response, "and all that sort of hocus-pocus stuff . . . Rumors, every one of them, quite naturally. And probably aggrandized, i.e. romanticized over the decades. However, I do gather that Tom was a decided loner—which doesn't sit well with your Cotswolds native. One of our neighbors also referred to him as 'handsome enough to be considered dangerous'—from which you may draw your own conclusions as to the speaker's motive—"

"Or the man's wife's," Judith threw in.

Angus raised an eyebrow. "Whereas Richard, the spouse in question, was a proper Oxford 'don' of the old school. My mind conjures up images of a stooped gent wreathed in perpetual pipe tobacco and clad in tweeds that have seen better days. Leather patches at the elbows, ink stains on his fingers, linen none too tidy. Not your ideal Lothario . . . Richard's specialty was fourteenth-century Venice; he was a well-respected scholar, but was also renowned for a barbed tongue and fearsome temper—"

"Supposedly a crossword fiend, too, Belle," Judith added.

"That's right," her husband said. "When he wasn't delving into the notorious Council of Ten and the infamous *Sbirri*—"

"Dinner's ready," Judith announced, and the two couples took their places at the table, murmuring appreciatively over the fare Judith had provided. "We're planning the traditional goose on Christmas," Angus announced. "And plum pudding, too."

"Angus is the 'bird' man," added his wife.

"Well, I can certainly use assistance. I'm not what you'd call a culinary virtuoso."

Wineglasses were raised and clinked. "Happy holidays, all."

"Christmas in the land of Charles Dickens. What a treat," Belle said. "And seeing your new home . . ."

"New to *us*, at any rate," Angus interjected.

The four sat in momentary silence as they took in the tranquil scene: deeply recessed windows leaded with diamond-shaped panes of glass, an oak-beamed ceiling darkened by decades of candlelight, floorboards worn and polished by the centuries, a fire crackling in a hearth that had once served as cook stove and roasting pit, the chill night air that whispered blackly outside the walls, making the room that much more inviting and companionable.

It was Belle who finally broke the magical spell. "So, there was a rumor that Katlin had a love affair with Tom?"

"Not in those words *per se,*" Angus responded slowly. "But I believe that was the general feeling hereabouts which, given Richard's intensely proud personality, must have been unendurable. He was a man of truly Victorian Era sensibilities. And for someone like that, being a suspected cuckold would have been—"

"Now who sounds Victorian?" Judith teased.

"At least I've made the transition into the twentieth century—"

"Except that we've entered the twenty-first—"

"Picky, picky."

"At least you're not time traveling with old Livius Andronicus," Judith said while Rosco asked a simple:

"Who?"

"Don't get him started, Rosco . . . We're talking 240 B.C. A former Greek slave turned Roman poet and dramaturge . . . Angus's latest scholarly work is a re-interpretation of Andronicus's Latin translation of the *Odyssey*."

"I see what you mean." Belle laughed, then changed the subject. "So . . . Richard, the purported 'crossword fiend'—"

"Aha!" burst in Angus. "I knew we'd get you hooked on our wee chronicle of suspense!"

Judith turned to Belle. "When we bought the house, we were told that after Katlin's disappearance, Richard became a regular hermit, even ordered the electric light shut off, and never ventured into town—"

Angus continued. "When Father Time finally came knocking, the house went vacant, and remained so for many, many years. Apparently, no one in the village wanted any part of it—"

"Some people even claimed it was haunted," Judith added.

"Quite a natural conjecture, too," her husband agreed. "It didn't help that the owner had been a

'Richard.' Too many brains jumped to allusions of King Richard III—the little princes locked away in the Tower, and all that other historical gore—"

Judith interrupted again. "It took two newcomer newlyweds to take a leap of faith and purchase the place. Angus *et moi* snagged it at a bargain price."

"Although it's not going to be any 'bargain' refurbishing these ancient walls, I can assure you." Across the candlelit table Angus gave his wife a smile.

"Elbow grease is all we need."

"*And* a pot of buried treasure if we're to accomplish the myriad renovations you've set your heart on."

"What became of the gardener in question?" Rosco asked after a moment.

It was Judith who answered. "Ah, here's where the plot really thickens. He also vanished without a trace."

Belle's gray eyes grew wide. "But wouldn't the police have immediately assumed that Richard—?"

"With no *corpora delecti*?" Angus replied. "And no substantive leads either? What could they possibly charge him with?"

"Katlin was American," Judy said. "Did we tell you that? Like me . . . Married to an Englishman—and a scholar."

Belle regarded her friend. "I trust you fare a good deal better."

Judith smiled again. "Oh, I am . . . I am . . ."

IT was that night that Belle found the crossword. Or rather a piece of one. Hand-drawn on a yellowed scrap of aged paper, the puzzle lay beside her nightclothes when she opened the dresser drawer. She picked it up, turning to show it to Rosco, but he'd disappeared into the bathroom. As she crossed the room, a sudden icy draft wafted across her shoulders. She shivered as the paper's thin corners fluttered in the agitated air, then grabbed a heavier sweater, tossing it hastily over her shoulders.

"You won't believe what I found," she called through the door that separated the "lav" from the bedroom.

"Is it black and white, and does it have letters and corresponding numbers?"

Belle laughed. "You know darn well it is . . . So, who put you up to this little trick? Angus or Judy, or both?"

Rosco reemerged. "Whatever they did, they did on their own."

Belle gave him a knowing glance, then concentrated on the crossword, perching on the bed as she did so. "You three have done yourself proud . . . This is quite intriguing . . ."

Rosco looked down at her, an amused smile on his face. "I thought you were complaining of jet lag toward the tail end of dinner."

Belle cocked her head to one side. "Is that a subtle hint?"

"I didn't think it was that subtle."

Belle laughed again, then dropped the torn word game on the nightstand. "You're right . . . Practical jokes can wait."

A Ghost of Christmas Past

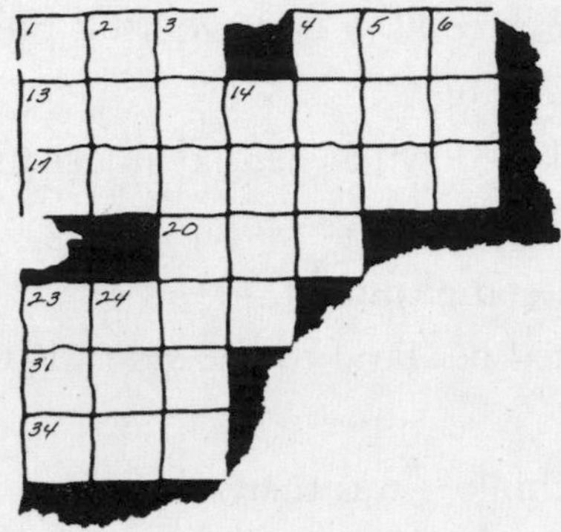

Across

1. *Bath, e.g.*
4. *"___on a Grecian Urn"*
7. *Siouan*
10. *Hostelry*
13. *Where C. Parr died*
15. *___Barrios, Sp.*
16. *Born*
17. *Rumpelstiltskin's rod*
18. *Alphabet starter*
19. *Past*
20. *London to Cambridge dir.*
21. *Certain title*
23. *Water, Sp.*

Down

1. *Snake sound*
2. *Small dog*
3. *"I"*
4. *"Ye___Sweet Shoppe"*
5. *Costa___Sol*
6. *Ogle*

A broad band of moonlight lay across the floor when she awakened, and her first inclination as she turned to gaze at its bright and steady line was to silently quote from Clement Clarke Moore's *A Visit from St. Nicholas*. "Not a creature was stirring . . ." Belle listened. No sound arose from the sleeping house or the quiescent village that lay beyond the windows. For someone accustomed to the wakeful energy of an American city—even in the midst of a winter night—the sheer lack of noise was almost unnerving.

She rubbed her foot against Rosco, who murmured dreamily before drifting back into peaceful slumber, then her gaze inadvertently moved to the nightstand and the torn crossword she'd left there. It was gone.

Belle sat up. She looked at the floor below the table. No scrap of paper lingered there. *That's curious*, she thought, and climbed out of bed, running her eyes over the uneven wooden boards and the hooked rug Judith was so proud to have found at a local flea market. No puzzle anywhere.

Suddenly a chill breeze assailed her. Belle turned indignantly toward the source. The swinging window sash she'd supposed had been shut fast was slowly opening inward. She hurried to the casement and pushed the offending panes of glass closed. A Tudor

Era house, sagging window frames, crooked floorboards—no wonder Judith and Angus were planning extensive renovations. Belle shook her head as she considered the magnitude of their project, then turned back toward the bed when suddenly the crossword fragment reappeared, sliding into a moonlit patch of flooring as though purposely blown there.

Okay, she thought. *I'll take the bait. Let's see what my hosts' crossword contains.*

She carried it into the bathroom, closing the door before switching on the overhead light. Then she spread the puzzle on the vanity, nodding in satisfaction as she began to admire her friends' ingenuity.

The paper was fragile, splotched, and brittle to the touch—obviously Judy and Angus had discovered a source for appropriately aged paper products, and the grid, hand-drawn in crackled brown ink, matched the timeworn motif. The tear had ripped along a line of darkened squares while the clues bore the graceful penmanship of an earlier era. As counterfeiters, Judy and Angus had done a remarkable job. *Now comes the true test,* Belle decided. *Are the clues as skillful as the packaging?*

She began to work, muttering to herself as she always did when faced with a linguistic conundrum. "1-

Across: *Bath*, e.g. . . . Three letters . . . 4-Across: '___ *on a Grecian Urn*.' " ODE, she wrote confidently while her thoughts kept rapid pace: *Ode on a Grecian Urn* . . . a poem by John Keats . . . An unlucky man in love . . . terribly jealous . . . hmmm . . . Could that be a subtle—or perhaps, not so subtle—reference to the mystery surrounding Judy and Angus's home? Katlin may have had a lover; Richard may have been a jealous husband? And of course, there was Angus's most recent area of study: an ancient Greek who wrote in Latin . . .

"Hmmm . . ." Belle mused aloud. "Hmmm . . ."

But at 13-Across she was stumped. The answer called for seven letters. The clue was *Where C. Parr died*. Her pen paused in midair; she vaguely remembered a dinner discussion centering around Henry VIII's last wife, and a local castle, but couldn't for the life of her recall the name.

Belle put down her pen. Kudos to Judy and Angus, she thought, especially for the interesting connection between a jealous lover and a dead queen . . . Catherine . . . Kate . . . Katlin . . . and Keats . . .

She tiptoed back into the bedroom, where another cold wind made her shiver. She spun toward the window. One panel was again wide open. Belle frowned in earnest as she crossed the room and forcibly closed it.

"YOU know I don't believe a word any of you are saying! I'm convinced you planted that puzzle fragment . . . besides, setting me up with a dinner conversation that alluded to your home's sinister past—not to mention other grisly stories. And the somewhat *obvious* suggestion that Richard was a crossword devotee . . . However, I've got to admit the torn paper and faded ink were terrific touches—"

"But we didn't—" Judith began, but Belle overrode her with a laughing:

"What I want to know is: was Rosco part of the plot back in the States, or did you only take him into your confidence last night . . . Or maybe this was his idea in the first place? No, I take back that suggestion. Judy, I've known you too long not to pin full blame on you. You may look innocent, but your old college pals will swear otherwise."

Additional protestations greeted Belle's teasing remarks. Ensconced in the rear seat beside Rosco while Angus drove and Judith provided a rapid travel commentary, Belle graced her friends—and her husband—with an amused wink.

"I especially appreciated the allusion to death vis-à-vis the clue about Catherine Parr and SUDELEY Castle . . . Oh, and the jealous lover reference with ODE . . . but you gave yourself away with the Greek bit, Angus, with all your palaver about Livius Andronicus—"

"So the crossword was in the dresser when you first spotted it?" was Angus's response.

"Of course, it was—as you well know." Belle chortled again and looked out the window. Despite the cold winter weather, England was still green, still miraculously verdant-looking. Wooly-coated cows and fluffier-looking sheep dotted pastures bisected by hedgerows from which burst sudden swarms of birds who spiraled in the air only to retreat to the safety of their shrubbery homes. "So, who was the author of the puzzle? Or was it a joint effort? Because I'm assuming it wasn't Rosco—not with all the British references."

It was Angus who answered. "None of us had a thing to do with it. I swear."

Belle began laughing outright. "If I didn't know better, Angus, I'd say you began your career on the stage. Besides, if you're arguing that you didn't construct the word game, then who am I supposed to believe *did* create it?"

"Maybe the puzzle fragment was in the dresser when you arrived," was Judy's serious response. "Some of the furniture came with the house. It's been here since, well . . . you know . . ."

"We're back to the haunted house routine, are we?"

"The puzzle has nothing to do with us, Belle!"

"Right . . ."

"Sudeley Castle!" Angus announced, swinging the auto into the car park.

"Perhaps you might consider doing a crossword-themed tour of 'ye olde England,' " Belle offered. "Fill in the clues at night . . . See aforementioned sites the next day."

"But we didn't—" Judith began.

"I'm going to get to the bottom of your little game," was Belle's cheery reply. "Don't think I'm as gullible as I look."

Rosco raised an eyebrow but chose to say nothing.

As they toured the grounds of Sudeley, Angus took the lead in detailing the history of the fifteenth-century stronghold. "You remember Thomas Seymour," he added almost as an afterthought, "the fellow who had matrimonial designs on Princess Elizabeth—later good Queen Bess . . . He was Baron Seymour of Sudeley, then; and when his project failed, he secretly wed Catherine Parr, King Henry VIII's widow. When *she* died, our ambitious Thomas renewed his pursuit of the future queen of England—"

"Thomas," Belle interrupted. "Ah . . . I see where this lecture is headed." She took Rosco's hand. "Okay, you three, I'll bite. We're back to our mystery crossword and the disappearance of your home's onetime owner . . . No, wait, I've got it . . . You're suggesting that Richard, having slaughtered—excuse the pun, I know Upper Slaughter's your hometown—that Richard killed his wife and perhaps her lover, said Thomas or Tom . . . then brought the bodies here and interred them on the grounds?"

"We're not suggesting any such thing!" was Judith's speedy reply while Angus grew pensive:

"An interesting proposition . . . Catherine Parr, survivor of a king who made it a habit of beheading his wives, marries a girlhood flame—as well as a former lover—then suddenly succumbs within her new home's walls . . ."

Belle stopped walking. "Would Richard have been aware of the story?"

"Of course." Angus also paused and thought.

"Well?" Belle looked from Angus to Judith, but it was Angus who replied.

"Sorry . . . Your theory of a clandestine burial won't wash . . . Sudeley's too public a spot."

Belle took her friends' hands. "You can both forsake the suspense stuff now. Rosco and I are having a wonderful time . . . You don't need to entertain us by inventing a crime that involves a crossword puzzle."

"But we didn't!"

In reply, Belle simply said, "What's next on the tour?"

"Minster Lovell Hall."

"Ah, yes, another deadly domicile . . ."

As they motored toward Minster Lovell Hall, passing through the villages of Stow-on-the-Wold and Chipping Norton with their medieval and half-timbered buildings, Belle found her thoughts returning to the vanished Katlin. She'd undoubtedly traveled this same route, probably walked and shopped the exact streets they were now driving over, and Belle began experiencing a curious empathy for the unknown woman. Had she been happily married or were the rumors of her infidelity true? And how had it been to live in this close-knit community as an ex-patriot? Perhaps even as the suspected intellectual inferior of a highly educated man?

" 'Chipping' meant 'cheapening' to our thirteenth-century forebears . . ." Belle was suddenly aware of Angus intoning in his most tutorial mode. ". . . thus indicating a market town . . . As you know, the Cotswolds region was the center for the nation's lucrative wool trade—"

It was Rosco who interrupted this narrative stream. "It's a shame there was no press coverage detailing Katlin's disappearance—or the resulting police activity."

Angus shifted the auto into a lower gear as he began merging with traffic entering a roundabout. "You've got to remember that reporters were tight-lipped in those days—both here and across the 'pond.' *Especially* when dealing with issues concerning conjecture and gossip."

Not like now, Belle was about to throw in, but didn't while Angus continued:

"Richard, difficult as he might have been, was a professor. One of the elite. Taught nearby, and all that.

Part of the established order . . . Whereas his wife was not only foreign, she was a ceramicist, and definitely a Bohemian sort, cozying up to gardeners and such like. Britain, in those days, was extraordinarily class conscious."

Judy suppressed a chuckle while Belle caught her friend's amused glance in the rearview mirror, and nodded in acknowledgment:

"None of Katlin's art remains, I take it?"

"Not in our house. Richard must have disposed of everything she made," Judy said.

Angus's face brightened. "You know . . . now, that you mention it . . . I remember seeing a small basin in an antiques shop in Burford. The design was sufficiently unusual that I inquired . . . I believe it had letters etched on it. The store's owner wasn't certain of the piece's provenance, but thought it had been done by the 'vanished lady.' What do you say we go for a look, and then have lunch? How about the Lamb Inn on Sheep Street, Judy? We can introduce Belle and Rosco to their traditional stilton pie—"

"And the smoked quail," his wife interjected.

Angus chortled. "Another extravagant 'terrine'—"

"The universe doesn't exist on steak and kidney pie anymore," his wife joked.

"Ah, for the bygone days of 'bangers and mash.' " He sighed dramatically.

"Was it difficult for you to settle in here, Judy?" was Belle's next query.

"You mean: have things changed since Katlin tried to win over the locals?"

Belle nodded.

"I've had a pretty easy go of it—despite the differences in Angus and my dining habits . . . But to answer you: no. I wouldn't have wanted to attempt Katlin's balancing act of 'town and gown.' Unless she had a stronger and more meaningful marriage than we suspect she had, I think Katlin must have been a lonely lady."

BURFORD'S High Street descended steeply to the meandering River Windrush. Shops selling woolens, expensive comestibles, and antiques were accommodated within stone Tudor Era buildings while the Norman bulk of St. John's Church dominated the town's riverside. Belle enjoyed the liveliness and palpable air of festivity: shoppers proudly carting Christmas gifts, children crowding in front of colorful window displays, parents smiling as they purchased "ice lollies" and other sweets. "What do you think, Rosco? Could we resettle here?"

"And forsake the fabled Polycrates family Tuesday night shoot-outs?"

"I assume you're talking about water pistols," offered Angus.

"Not even," was Rosco's quick response. "But you take a bunch of Greek-Americans—"

"Even though they're all from the same family—" chimed in Belle while Rosco finished with a wry:

"Let's just say things can get pretty hairy."

"Ah, for the Wild West," said Angus.

"I'd hardly call Massachusetts 'west,' " his wife rejoined.

"Well, west of here." Then Angus prepared to launch into another historical monologue. "The community you see before you has existed as long as there's been an England . . . In fact, the remnants of a Roman statuette appear within the church walls while a Celtic settlement prospered on the Windrush's banks well before Julius Caesar invaded—"

"Where's this famous pottery bowl?" Belle and Judith interrupted in unison.

* * *

HALF hidden on the lower shelf of an out-of-the-way display rack, the piece in question was cerulean blue, the color surprisingly modern and bold. Fierce yellow letters gleamed through the glaze, circling and recircling two entwining messages: *Semper et Ubique, Ora e Sempre.* Belle held the bowl in her hands while the shop owner needlessly translated:

" 'Always and Everywhere' in Latin . . . 'Now and Forever' in Italian . . . It's quite an eye-catching article . . . Not to everyone's taste, however . . . As I said, I can't vouch for its history—"

"But it's purported to have been the work of the 'vanished lady'?" Belle asked.

"That's the rumor."

Belle turned the piece over; on the rim was a minute and faintly carved "for R." She paid the asking price without another question.

"For Rosco?" her husband jibed.

"Dream on," she said.

WHILE Judith, Angus, and Rosco unpacked groceries and began parsing out tasks for dinner's preparation, Belle carried her prize up to the guest room, then yelped in surprise as she opened the door. Another crossword segment was blowing lazily across the floor beneath the window. She placed Katlin's bowl on the dresser, and bent to retrieve the puzzle, noting again the fastidious use of distressed paper and faded ink as she scanned the clues. Belle smiled to herself, then left the bedroom and headed down the stairs.

" 'What news on the Rialto?' " Angus announced as she entered the kitchen.

"It's a clever game," she answered. "But you can stop now." She handed Angus the puzzle segment. "I mean it."

Instead of replying, her host scrutinized the crossword. "46-Down," he murmured. "Three letters . . . ____*castle* . . . lowercase. NEW*castle*?"

Judith peered around her husband's shoulder. "62-Down . . . three letters . . . ____*long you'll know the truth* . . . Could that be ERE?"

"Okay, you two," Belle said. "Stop. I'm serious—"

"But it isn't us, Belle." Two very sincere faces regarded her while Rosco joined in with an equally earnest:

"It's not a trick, Belle . . . or a practical joke."

Belle frowned. "But if you all didn't . . ."

In response, Angus uttered a pensive, "Let's take a walk. We need to clear our brains."

A Ghost of Christmas Past

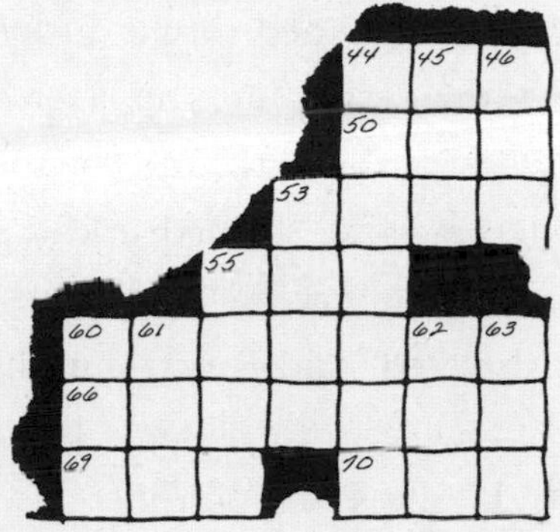

Across
44. American fiver
47. A___land
49. Certain cars
50. High card
51. Logical lead-in?
52. Scottish cap
53. Sprouted
54. Minster Lovell___
55. Havana Mrs.
56. 24-Down foe
58. 4-Down updated
60. Encumbent
64. Crew
65. Irish grp.
66. ___Falls
67. Unusual
68. Evanston, Ill. sch.
69. Canadian prov.
70. Evergreen

Down
45. Chill
46. ___castle
48. Borrowed
53. Pirate quaff
55. Quarrel
56. Pigeon noise
57. Unhappy
59. Muslim month Lead-in
60. Greek yod
61. Writer Anais
62. "___long, you'll learn the truth"
63. Uncooked

They strolled the mile-long footpath connecting the villages of Lower and Upper Slaughter. The wintry afternoon had now darkened into a dusky gray-green; the birds had grown still, but the river continued to whistle noisily beside the path, and the sound, perhaps heightened by the dark, seemed oddly sinister as if drowned voices were crying out from the water's depths. Belle shivered, and Rosco put an arm around her shoulder.

"I'm not cold," she said. "I'm just . . . well, I don't know . . ."

"Spooked?" he asked.

"I guess that's it."

"Me too," Judith agreed. "The idea of our house being haunted gives me the willies, but I don't know what else—"

"But there must be a logical explanation," Angus protested. "You just don't have ghosts scribbling away on scraps of paper—"

"That's what happens in seances," his wife argued.

"Judith, you're not going to tell me you believe in that malarkey." His tone was surprisingly edgy.

"All I know is that two pieces of a crossword appeared out of the blue—"

"Hey, you two!" Belle said, "No bickering allowed . . . Let's back up and examine the situation."

"I agree with Angus," Rosco added. "There has to be a logical—"

"Okay, I found the first puzzle fragment in the dresser when I reached in to grab my pajamas—"

"Meaning we'd already unpacked, and hadn't seen hide nor hair of it—"

"Which is why I assumed you guys had planted it," Belle concluded.

Rosco turned to Angus, his brow lined in concentration. "The dresser was in the room when you purchased the house . . . Isn't that what you told us?" As Angus nodded, Rosco continued, "Okay, bear with me for a moment . . . You said the police 'assumed' Katlin had been killed—even without *corpora delecti*? And Tom, too? Did they believe he'd been the victim of foul play as well?"

"Yes . . . at least, according to our neighbors," was Judith's pensive response.

"Okay . . . going under the assumption that Katlin and Tom were killed, there would be remains . . . But you stated none were found . . . Which seems strange . . . Wouldn't someone have discovered the corpses by now—a new homeowner adding an outbuilding or an addition? Sixty years is a long time, and the area is much more populous than it was."

"Not if the bodies were buried in a secluded area—or one that's off-limits," Angus said. "We took you to Minster Lovell today . . . Hailes Abbey is also a nearby ruin: nothing but undisturbed greensward and moss-covered walls. It's a designated landmark, a museum by day, but often a trysting spot at night."

"A trysting spot," Belle said. "Tryst . . . a Middle English word from the Old French *triste* meaning 'watching post' . . . while modern French translates *triste* as 'sad' . . . And Slaughter, on top of it all—"

"The villages' names aren't what you think," Angus offered. "The word's a corruption of the Saxon *sloh* meaning a 'marshy place.' "

She turned to regard him. "But the Old English word for 'slaughter' is *sleaht*, from *slean*, 'to slay'—"

Judith stared. "How do you know arcane facts like these?"

"I'd like to tell you I have Old and Middle English at my fingertips . . . But the truth is, I looked it up when you asked us to visit. Not the tryst part, though . . ." Belle drew in a thoughtful breath, then changed the subject. "What if Richard discovered the two lovers at Minster Lovell or Hailes Abbey or another secluded trysting place, and then—"

Rosco interrupted her. "This is purely hypothetical . . . but is it possible that Richard was our crossword's constructor?"

Belle frowned. "You mean he created the puzzle as a kind of final confession?" She shook her head. "But then how do you explain the fact that it was hidden? What purpose would it serve if no one knew it existed?"

"Angus said the man was eccentric . . . maybe even crazy. People like that do irrational things."

"I don't know," said Belle. "If the man was lucid enough to construct a crossword—"

"No, I get what Rosco's driving at," put in Angus. "A message intended to outlast Richard's death . . . That type of delusional behavior would be consistent with a mind teetering on insanity . . . Perhaps Richard committed his heinous crime and then repented, and the puzzle was his means of—"

"Or," Rosco interrupted, "maybe the crossword is a kind of perverted treasure map."

Belle spun toward her husband. "You mean: leading the puzzle's finder to the spot the bodies are buried?"

"Could be."

All four broke into an immediate jog, hurrying along the path toward Judith and Angus's home.

ENTERING the house, Belle raced up the stairs and began dumping the contents of the dresser drawers on her bed. Rosco, Judith, and Angus were close on her heels.

"When I found the first crossword segment, the window had blown open . . . There was another draft today . . ." Belle ran her hand through the chest's cavities. "If the puzzle had been taped inside, I might have dislodged it when I unpacked. Then a breeze entered through a crack in the old wood . . . I should have considered this possibility earlier."

Angus and Rosco moved forward, and together they upended the chest and carefully searched the interior with a "torch."

Nothing. All hands came away empty. All faces were equally dispirited.

The four straightened up and stared at each other. "But how—" Belle began when she suddenly spotted a fragment of paper lying half-hidden under the bed. Without uttering a sound, she leaped toward it and retrieved the third and final piece of the puzzle from the floor. "Roman numerals beginning at 3-Down and ending at 44-Down . . . A seven-part message . . ." she said in an awed whisper as she slid the three separate pieces together. *"I, II, III, IV, V, VI, VII . . ."*

The two couples marched solemnly down to the dining room, where Angus, Judy, and Rosco huddled at Belle's back as she breathlessly filled in clues. The only sounds were the creak of floorboards and her hand moving swiftly over the table top. 38-Across: *What evil men do with good women* . . . 54-Across: *Minster Lovell* ____. Belle penned in HALL, then returned her attention to an earlier clue: 37-Across: *March date.* "When did Katlin disappear?" she asked as she wrote IDES.

Angus and Judith looked at each other. "I think it was spring—" he began, then bent closer to Belle's shoulder as he pointed to 65-Across. "*Irish grp.* . . . Three letters . . . AOH is my hunch: the abbreviation for Ancient Order of Hibernia. And 7-Down, also three letters, *Siberian town*, beginning with an O; that might be OLA. Whoever concocted this crossword possessed a goodly intellect."

Judith drew in her breath with a nervous sigh. "I

liked it better when we didn't know for certain what became of Katlin . . ." Her voice trailed off; she glanced apprehensively across the room as her friend continued to work.

Finally, Belle sat back and stared at the waiting threesome. She'd circled each part of the message with her red pen, and the pen trembled in her hand.

"To think the villagers never uncovered the—" Judith murmured at length.

Her husband agreed. "It seems painfully obvious now, doesn't it?"

The two couples continued gazing at the crossword. At last, Rosco gave voice to the question all were thinking. "But why create a puzzle instead of simply writing a letter?"

Judith's voice was soft. "Could it have been a delaying tactic? Or perhaps a means to forestall pain?"

"But I go back to my original query," Belle said. "If no one was aware of the crossword's existence, what good was it?"

"And why did it reappear after all these decades?" Judith continued. "And why was it ripped in thirds?"

It was Rosco who proposed an answer. "Maybe the paper simply broke along lines containing the heaviest concentration of ink . . . Or desperate hands could have torn it, then tossed it into the dresser—fully intending to keep the message hidden." He paused. "We could be facing a situation as logical as that . . ."

Belle moved the crossword segments apart, then reunited them. "Logical," she echoed. "I suppose—" A noise stopped the words in her throat. Upstairs, the guest room window had blown open and shut with a violent, heavy bang.

"If you don't believe in ghosts," she murmured.

"Richard's?" Angus asked.

"Katlin's," was Belle's quiet response.

Across

1. Bath, e.g.
4. "___on a Grecian Urn"
7. Siouan
10. Hostelry
13. Where C. Parr died
15. ___Barrios, Sp.
16. Born
17. Rumpelstiltskin's rod
18. Alphabet starter
19. Past
20. London to Cambridge dir.
21. Certain title
23. Water, Sp.
25. Doctrine
28. Christmas decoration
31. Male sheep
32. Town on the Meuse
33. Kalita's son
34. Attempt
35. Shade maker
37. March date
38. What evil men do with good women
40. Equal, comb. form
43. Salutes
44. American fiver
47. A___land
49. Certain cars
50. High card
51. Logical lead-in?
52. Scottish cap
53. Sprouted
54. Minster Lovell___
55. Havana Mrs.
56. 24-Down foe
58. 4-Down updated
60. Encumbent
64. Crew
65. Irish grp.
66. ___Falls
67. Unusual
68. Evanston, Ill. sch.
69. Canadian prov.
70. Evergreen

Down

1. Snake sound
2. Small dog
3. "I"
4. "Ye___Sweet Shoppe"
5. Costa___Sol
6. Ogle
7. Siberian town
8. "V"
9. Future King of Sweden?
10. "VI"
11. Not pos.
12. New, comb. form
14. Sicilian town
22. Double-check the gun
23. Mona Lisa, e.g.
24. Lincoln's Men; Abbr.
25. "III"
26. Domingo or Antonio
27. "IV"
29. Knot
30. ___Royal Highness
32. Big___house
36. Confused
38. "___twinkle in his eye."
39. Road curve

A Ghost of Christmas Past

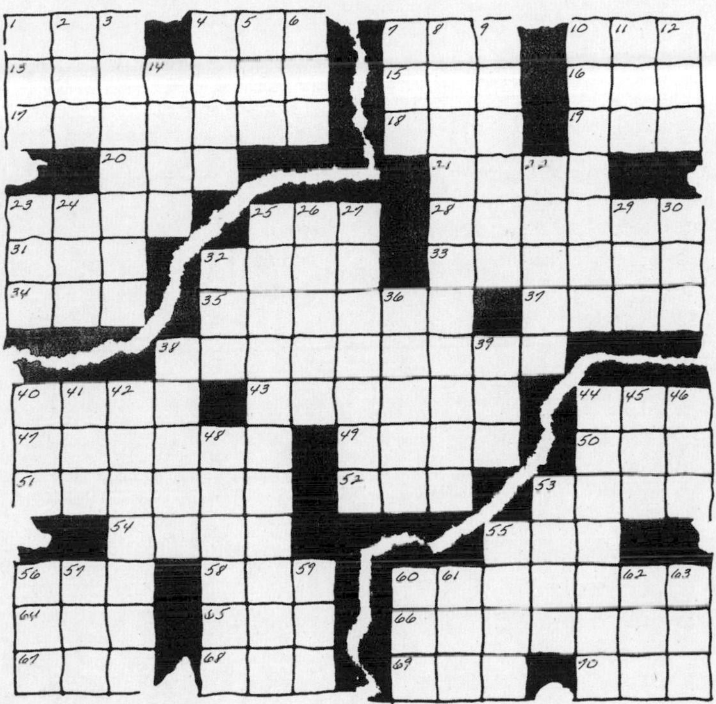

40. Attention getter
41. Gorilla, e.g.
42. "II"
44. "VII"
45. Chill
46. ___castle
48. Borrowed
53. Pirate quaff
55. Quarrel
56. Pigeon noise
57. Unhappy
59. Muslim month lead-in
60. Greek god
61. Writer Anais
62. "___long, you'll learn the truth"
63. Uncooked

The Answers

A Crossworder's Holiday

1 S	2 L	3 A	4 T	■	■	■	5 F	6 A	7 R	■	8 S	9 P	10 A	11 R
12 C	A	S	I	13 O	■	14 R	A	R	A	■	15 T	A	L	E
16 I	C	H	A	N	17 G	E	D	M	Y	18 R	U	L	E	S
19 S	E	E	■	20 L	O	N	■	■	21 S	O	D	■	■	■
■	■	■	22 P	A	G	E	23 R	■	■	24 L	I	25 P	26 P	27 O
28 F	29 O	30 U	R	N	O	W	A	31 R	32 E	F	O	O	L	S
33 R	U	N	E	D	■	■	34 I	O	N	■	■	35 R	A	M
36 E	T	A	S	■	37 H	38 E	N	C	E	■	39 A	T	N	O
40 D	O	M	■	■	41 R	E	B	■	■	42 E	P	I	C	S
43 A	N	O	44 A	45 T	H	L	O	46 R	47 D	D	R	A	K	E
48 S	E	R	R	A	■	■	49 W	A	I	L	S	■	■	■
■	■	■	50 C	C	51 P	■	■	52 Z	E	E	■	53 W	54 S	55 W
56 Y	57 O	58 U	H	O	L	59 D	60 N	O	T	A	61 F	A	K	E
62 E	L	S	E	■	63 O	N	E	R	■	64 R	A	D	A	R
65 A	D	E	S	■	66 T	A	T	■	■	■	67 T	E	T	E

The Proof of the Pudding

1 E	2 L	3 L	■	4 R	5 A	6 F	■	7 B	8 E	9 E	■	10 T	11 I	12 E
13 L	I	B	■	14 A	L	I	■	15 A	L	L	■	16 O	N	E
17 I	N	O	■	18 C	A	N	19 D	I	E	D	20 P	E	E	L
21 J	A	F	22 F	E	■	23 N	U	T	M	E	G	■	■	■
24 A	G	R	O	■	25 M	E	N	■	■	26 S	A	27 C	28 K	29 S
30 H	E	A	R	31 S	A	Y	■	32 P	33 E	T	■	34 U	L	E
■	■	35 I	G	O	R	■	36 R	R	R	■	37 U	P	O	N
38 E	39 S	S	E	N	C	40 E	O	F	A	41 L	M	O	N	D
42 P	H	I	S	■	43 I	D	I	■	44 S	E	L	F	■	■
45 I	O	N	■	46 T	A	D	■	47 T	E	N	A	B	48 L	49 E
50 C	O	S	51 B	Y	■	■	52 F	I	R	■	53 U	R	A	L
■	■	■	54 C	L	55 O	56 V	E	S	■	57 S	T	A	V	E
58 B	59 L	60 A	D	E	O	F	M	A	61 C	E	■	62 N	O	V
63 I	T	S	■	64 R	O	W	■	65 N	O	R	■	66 D	R	E
67 S	D	S	■	68 S	S	S	■	69 E	B	B	■	70 Y	O	N

A Partridge in a Pear Tree

1 A	2 M	3 I	4 S	5 S		6 W	7 A	8 D		9 A	10 M	11 I	12 G	13 O
14 R	A	L	P	H		15 I	R	A		16 L	E	D	O	N
17 A	L	L	I	O	18 W	N	I	D	19 O	L	E	A	V	E
			20 T	R	O	D			21 N	E	T			
22 H	23 A	24 M		25 N	O	O	26 N	27 D	A	Y		28 B	29 R	30 O
31 U	P	O	32 N			33 W	O	E			34 S	E	E	D
35 T	O	M	Y	36 N	37 E	P	H	E	38 W	39 S	T	E	V	E
			40 S	O	D	A		41 P	A	I	R			
42 A	43 L	44 A	S	D	O	N	45 O	T	G	R	I	46 E	47 V	48 E
49 H	O	Y	A			50 E	A	R			51 P	L	A	N
52 A	T	E		53 M	54 I	S	T	O	55 O	56 K		57 L	T	D
			58 A	E	R			59 U	S	E	60 R			
61 T	62 I	63 S	F	A	T	64 E	65 I	B	E	L	I	66 E	67 V	68 E
69 O	N	E	A	L		70 M	I	L		71 S	P	R	E	E
72 O	N	E	R	S		73 T	I	E		74 O	S	A	G	E

Mum's the Word

		1 B	2 E	3 E	4 F				5 S	6 P	7 A	8 T		
	9 T	A	C	T	I	10 C		11 S	C	A	T	H	12 E	
13 J	A	N	U	A	R	Y		14 M	U	M	M	E	R	15 S
16 O	L	D			17 S	P	18 I	E	L			19 S	R	A
20 E	L	I		21 S	T	R	O	L	L	22 S		23 P	O	T
24 L	O	T	25 S	A		26 U	R	L		27 C	28 H	O	R	E
	29 W	O	O	D	30 Y	S		31 S	32 C	O	O	T	S	
			33 U	F	O				34 O	R	S			
	35 M	36 U	T	A	N	37 T		38 M	E	E	T	39 M	40 E	
41 E	I	G	H	T		42 A	43 V	A		44 R	A	R	E	45 R
46 S	N	L		47 E	48 X	P	I	R	49 E	S		50 I	R	A
51 Q	U	I			52 R	E	E	K	S			53 M	I	G
54 S	T	E	55 L	56 L	A	R		57 E	S	58 C	59 A	P	E	E
	60 E	S	S	A	Y	S		61 T	E	A	S	E	R	
		62 T	T	Y	S				63 S	A	K	I		

A Ghost of Christmas Past

1 S	2 P	3 A	■	4 O	5 D	6 E	■	7 O	8 T	9 O	■	10 I	11 N	12 N
13 S	U	D	14 E	L	E	Y	■	15 L	O	S	■	16 N	E	E
17 S	P	I	N	D	L	E	■	18 A	B	C	■	19 A	G	O
■	■	20 E	N	E	■	■	■	■	21 E	A	22 R	L	■	■
23 A	24 G	U	A	■	25 I	26 S	27 M	■	28 W	R	E	A	29 T	30 H
31 R	A	M	■	32 A	M	A	Y	■	33 I	V	A	N	I	I
34 T	R	Y	■	35 S	U	N	H	36 A	T	■	37 I	D	E	S
■	■	■	38 W	A	S	T	E	T	H	39 E	M	■	■	■
40 P	41 A	42 R	I	■	43 T	O	A	S	T	S	■	44 F	45 I	46 N
47 S	P	I	T	48 O	F	■	49 R	E	O	S	■	50 A	C	E
51 T	E	C	H	N	O	■	52 T	A	M	■	53 G	R	E	W
■	■	54 H	A	L	L	■	■	■	■	55 S	R	A	■	■
56 C	57 S	A	■	58 O	L	59 D	■	60 I	61 N	P	O	W	62 E	63 R
64 O	A	R	■	65 A	O	H	■	66 N	I	A	G	A	R	A
67 O	D	D	■	68 N	W	U	■	69 O	N	T	■	70 Y	E	W

About the Authors

NERO BLANC is the nom de plume of novelists Cordelia Frances Biddle and Steve Zettler, who also happen to be husband and wife. They invite you to visit them at their website: www.crosswordmysteries.com, where you can find information on other books in the Nero Blanc series. They love hearing from their fans.